DANGEROUS TIDINGS

DANA MENTINK

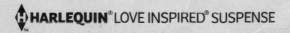

HARLEQUIN® LOVE INSPIRED® SUSPENSE

Recycling programs
for this product may
not exist in your area.

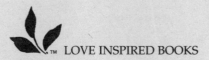

™ LOVE INSPIRED BOOKS

ISBN-13: 978-0-373-44705-3

Dangerous Tidings

Copyright © 2015 by Dana Mentink

www.Harlequin.com

Printed in U.S.A.

This is love: not that we loved God, but that he loved us
and sent his Son as an atoning sacrifice for our sins.
—1 John 4:10

To the One who left the throne to walk among us.

ONE

Dark shadows drifted across the tiny office window. Even the lights strung along the ferryboat across the way could not chase away Donna Gallagher's tickle of unease as she gazed out at San Diego Bay. Rain beaded on the glass, a winter storm. The vessel was already crowded in spite of the weather. In the upcoming three weeks, the number of visitors would swell as eager Christmas shoppers came over from the mainland and overnight guests arrived for the Hotel del Coronado's holiday festival. Twinkling white lights, ice-skating, fireworks and hot cocoa. The perfect Christmas in the beautiful island town of Coronado.

Every year since she could remember, her father, Bruce, had accompanied Donna, her three sisters and their mother to the festival. Every year, until now.

The pain in her chest started up again and tears pricked her eyelids. In the corner of the office stood a small pine tree, decorated with handmade ornaments. Each daughter had taken great pains to craft the perfect ornament for their father's office tree, except two years ago when Donna hadn't made one. The unfairness of it burned in her. This year, she was fully recovered and ready to make up for lost time. It was the holiday that would finally erase her disastrous rebellion, bury it firmly under a pile of happy memories.

The Gallaghers were all healthy, Candace finally on her feet after her husband's death in Afghanistan five years prior and Donna recovered from the crash, physically, anyway.

She had not yet put the finishing touches on her wooden cable car, a remembrance of their trip to San Francisco, where she'd turned back to God and decided to start living again, thanks to her father. But now it was too late. Christmas held no joy for Donna this year, and she wondered if it ever would again.

Besides the grief, something dark and frightening poked at her instincts. Bruce, her father, her hero, had been murdered, she was certain of it. All around her, on every inch of floor and the sleek wooden tabletop, lay stacks of files that she'd extracted from the cabinet. The answer to his death lay inside, she was positive. Wind rattled the office windows. She jumped.

She could not shake the sensation that someone was watching her, waiting to make sure she didn't find her answers. Paranoia? Exhaustion? Her sisters would probably say both. They thought she was in denial, her imagination exacerbated by grief and stress. And guilt, her heart added. There was no murder, they insisted, just an accident.

And her impulse to sift through her father's cases and play the part of a private investigator, as he had been?

A ludicrous attempt to take control of her grief. She was a veterinarian, after all, not a detective. But ever since she'd started looking through Bruce Gallagher's paperwork, there had been hints of danger.

Nerves, she told herself. The vehicle that appeared in her rearview mirror too often, the repeated hang-up phone calls on the office line. She looked out onto the darkened street. A truck drove slowly along, pulling to the curb outside. Was it the same truck she'd imagined was following her? Heart thudding, she stood behind the screen of the curtain, watching. A soft glow from inside, the flicker from a cigarette. Who would stop for a smoke here? Stomach tight, she watched.

One long minute and the vehicle drove away. The breath whooshed out of her. *Paranoid, Donna.*

She picked up her father's most recent file from the "active" tray on his desk. The neat label, Mitchell, P., rang a bell deep down in her memory. Mitchell, P. Her memory supplied the full name. Pauline Mitchell.

It was not Pauline's face that sprang into her mind but the face of Radar, her German shepherd. Something ticked up deep in Donna's stomach. She'd treated Radar a month earlier, and when she'd called to check on the dog's improvement a few days later, there had been no answer and no return of her messages.

Inside the file there was only one sheet of paper, adorned with her father's nearly microscopic handwriting.

Her eyes wandered to the small picture on the desk— Bruce, in his marine dress uniform, arm slung rakishly around his wife, JeanBeth. What had her father's interest been in Pauline Mitchell? She must have been a client, but as far as Donna had known, they'd never met.

The office phone rang, shattering the silence and jolting her nerves. Too late for a business call. She blinked hard and went to switch off the ringer.

But what if it was the hospital calling about Sarah? Her youngest sister was stable now, the doctors assured her. Safe after being pried from behind the wheel in the crash that had killed their father.

She reached to pick it up, stopping in uncertainty until the message kicked in. "Pacific Coast Investigations. Please leave a number and I'll return your call." Her father's voice on the recording nearly took the knees from under her. There was the obligatory beep and then a long pause. Could she hear breathing on the other end of the line? She was not certain. The caller ID was unfamiliar. Wrong number?

She picked it up. "Hello? Who is this?"

Silence. There was someone on the line, she was sure. The same person who'd called and hung up a dozen times. "I said, who is this?"

Click.

A creak from the hallway brought her to her feet.

"Calm down, already," she chided herself.

It was Marco, no doubt, her father's business partner and a longtime family friend. He had a key and came and went as he pleased. She heaved out a sigh. Now nearly forty, Marco was a former Navy boxing world champion, and she did not have to worry about her safety while he was around. Marco loved her and her three sisters as if they were his own kin, even if her relationship with Marco had been downright prickly at times. He was grieving the loss of Bruce Gallagher, too.

She picked up the file again and the paper slipped out and fell to the floor. She bent over to retrieve it. A shadow flitted through her peripheral vision.

She froze.

Her paranoia again?

Or was someone else there in the empty office?

It was her imagination, she decided, until she heard the creak of a floorboard.

Brent Mitchell finally felt his muscles loosen. The run had eased the nervous energy that cascaded through him. Even though the coast guard doctor had firmly cautioned him to take things slow during his recovery, Brent figured the four-mile jog fit the bill, since he'd normally run six. The rain didn't slow him down. Instead, it washed the Southern California air so clean it almost hurt to breathe it.

Another ten to twelve days of leave from his job to rest from a concussion might as well have been an eternity, and a short run seemed like a better option than going slowly insane. Besides, he could not lose a twist in his gut, that same sensation that he'd gotten just before the last time he'd dropped from a helicopter into a heaving ocean. Something wasn't quite right. He checked his phone again. No messages.

There were plenty of reasons why his sister, Pauline, might have split town for a while, leaving calls unanswered. She could be mad at him, which he richly deserved. He was probably in the running for the "worst brother of the year" award. Still, he felt a niggle in his gut. Pauline had a temper, but she was also quick to forgive and this period of radio silence had lasted longer than usual. He'd even gone so far as to let himself into her house, but found nothing out of place. Still, the uneasiness continued, so he'd snatched up an address tacked to her bulletin board and followed it to the front walkway of a neatly tended little building on Coronado Island at eleven thirty on a crisp December night.

His cell phone vibrated. "Brent Mitchell."

No answer at first. "Where...where is she?"

He stiffened. "Who are you looking for?"

The breath on the other end was short, panicky. Click. Disconnect.

Brent stared at the phone. Wrong number? Or someone who was also looking for his sister? He pushed Redial and waited. Endless ringing. No answer.

Focus on the now, he told himself, though his nerves were firing like a rifle volley. *Follow up on that call later.*

Of course the business he'd sought out was closed, dark, except for dim light that shone through the shutters upstairs. Nothing out of the ordinary, except maybe for the beat-up truck parked in front. Not a neighborhood for trashy vehicles.

He headed up the walkway to read the lettering on the front window just as a big man with a crew cut stepped out from the shadows.

"Help you?"

His arms were muscled, damp with sweat, as if he, too,

had been out for a run. He kept his hands loose, slightly away from his body, alert. Coronado Island was home to North Island Naval Air Station and across the water from Brent's own coast guard base. The area was thick with military types. This guy could be anyone from a navy SEAL to a petty officer. Brent figured the guy was too old to be petty officer, and, since it was just plain stupid to antagonize a navy SEAL, he tried for a friendly tone. Brent could be a smart-mouth, but he didn't have a death wish. "Just out for a run."

"In the rain?"

"That's the best time to run. The tourists are all inside." He shot a look at the darkened building. "What kind of business is this?"

"Why do you want to know?"

Brent raised an eyebrow. "Why shouldn't I?"

"You're trespassing." The man eased forward a little.

Brent tensed but did not back down. If it was going to come down to something physical, he wouldn't run from it. "Public place."

"Private property."

The obstinate mule inside him kicked to life. "You don't own this sidewalk and it's an innocent enough question. Don't see why you've got your back up about it."

The guy looked him up and down. "You're persistent. Navy?"

"Coast guard."

A slight derogatory smile. "Puddle jumper, huh?"

Brent answered through gritted teeth. "Rescue swimmer."

He humphed, but there was a slight relaxing in the posture. "Knew a coastie swimmer."

"Yeah?"

"Got my buddy out of a jam after Katrina hit. You work that mess?"

"Fifteen saves in one night." Including a three-day-old infant whose panicked father had shoved the baby into Brent's arms while they were in a rescue basket at 150 feet in the air and Brent was struggling to operate the hoist. His fingers tensed automatically with the memory. That fragile life in his hands. All on him whether the child lived or died.

They stayed silent a moment.

Brent jutted his chin. "You military?"

"Navy."

"Swabbie, huh?"

No smile this time.

"I worked Katrina, too. Helped out building Camp Lucky. Know it?"

Brent nodded. It was the makeshift facility built by the military to collect the animals rescued from the hurricane. "We pulled out a golden retriever who ended up there. There were plenty we couldn't get." Plenty of helpless lives all around him then. They'd lost people and animals alike. It stuck in his craw.

The big man shook his head and Brent saw that he, too, understood about rescues gone bad. Losses that neither one of them would admit to.

"Wanted to take all those animals home with me."

Something squeezed tight inside Brent. Pauline had said the same thing after the Loma Prieta quake when she'd helped with rescue efforts and come home with Radar. He straightened. "Brent Mitchell."

"Marco."

"You always this hostile to passersby?"

"We've had some trouble."

"Do tell."

Marco remained silent, no doubt weighing how much to confide. The sensation in Brent's gut kicked up a notch. Trouble seemed to be going around.

Where is she? The desperate voice stuck in his mind.

"That your ride there?" Marco gestured to the truck parked at the curb.

"Nope. Came on foot."

"Got to go check something out." Marco turned, stopping to throw a comment over his shoulder. "We're a private investigation business. Now get lost, Coastie." He took off at a brisk walk toward the building.

Private investigation? Why had Pauline been interested in such a service?

Where is she?

He mulled it over for a minute. Good sense would dictate that a guy with a concussion, confronted by a burly navy type, should turn around and go home. Then again, normal men with common sense would not dive into the heart of a raging ocean in high winds to snatch up a victim moments away from death. Pauline always said he had a decided lack of good sense.

Semper Paratus was the coast guard motto.

Always Ready.

"Ready or not," he said under his breath as he followed.

Donna whirled around so fast she upset the empty water pitcher she'd left on the table. It clattered to the floor but did not break. She ignored it, still tingling with fear over what she'd thought she'd seen out of the corner of her eye behind the bank of file cabinets. The creak of the floor had not repeated itself. Her eyes were playing tricks. Must be.

The cell phone shook in her hands as her finger hovered on the buttons to call 911. Breath in her throat, she tiptoed toward the cabinets. She crept slowly until she got within a step of the cabinet's edge, then quickly poked her head around, ready to summon help.

No one. She heaved out a breath. There was no one

there in the office, save one silly, frightened, grief-stricken twenty-seven-year-old woman.

Her sisters were right. Her mountain of sorrow and regret was causing her to imagine things. She retrieved the pitcher and walked it back to the conference room, the file folder tucked under her arm. She settled into a chair at the side. The head of the table would always be her father's spot. Her throat thickened. Had it really been only two weeks since he was sitting there, strong and solid, thumbing through files and drinking the ultra-strong coffee he enjoyed? Only two weeks of anguish and grief so strong she'd had to take a leave from her veterinary practice? The Gallagher family had spent endless hours listening to the detailed police findings. It was an accident that took their father's Lexus over the guardrail and down a rocky slope along Highway 1. Days had been spent wondering whether Sarah would recover and watching their mother remain at Sarah's bedside, deep in prayer.

Suppose they were right and it had been an accident. Sarah, the driver, had been rear ended, causing the Gallagher's car to plunge over the side. The other driver had not stopped. Maybe Sarah would regain her memory of the accident and confirm that it had been nothing more than a horrible, tragic mistake.

But something did not feel right—she had the feeling she got sometimes when a dog's symptoms told one story but her gut supplied another. Odd that the driver had not stopped to call for help.

Before his death, her normally cheerful father had been preoccupied, working late hours, investigating some case that he had not wanted to discuss.

Or, she thought with a pang of guilt, had they all been too busy to listen? She had her own career, her sister Sarah had a busy life as a surgical nurse, and Candace was grieving over the loss of her marine husband with a child to raise. Most worrying of all was Navy Chaplain Angela, struggling to recover from a devastating tour in Afghanistan.

They'd all been happy that Bruce Gallagher had started up his private investigation service. It gave him purpose, and he'd enjoyed solving cases only for people with military connections. It filled that part of his soul that had never stopped being a marine. *Semper Fidelis* was not just a motto to her father. He had been faithful to his family and the corps until the last moment of his life. He'd always done the right thing, the difficult thing, even when she'd openly despised him for it.

She opened the file again. She'd removed the folders from the cabinet methodically and this was the only one from the drawer labeled Current that she had not gone through thoroughly. Pauline Mitchell's file. Inside, there was only a list of names.

Curious.

The others were crammed full of statements, detailed bank information and even photographs, but this one had nothing except a list of names.

3. Darius Fields
2. Jeff Kinsey
1. Brent Mitchell

The shadow caught her eye. Her head jerked toward the door. Again, nothing. Only the pounding of her heart, the rasping of her own breath. Then she thought she caught the sound of someone moving along the front walkway. Clutching the file in her hand, she shot to her feet. She'd lock the door to put her mind at ease.

As she pushed the chair out, a man's hand reached from under the table and wrapped around her ankle, the fingers slick with sweat.

TWO

Brent trailed a step behind Marco as they sprinted up the steps. He finally caught the name on the front window as he passed.

Pacific Coast Investigations.

Why hadn't Pauline mentioned it? His heart sped up a notch, but there was no time to indulge the feeling. They arrived in a well-appointed office cluttered with files. A Christmas tree occupied the corner, and he caught a whiff of pine.

Marco scanned the room.

"What are you looking for?"

"Thought I told you to beat it."

"I don't take orders from swabbies."

Marco's eyes swiveled to the conference room just as the door slammed shut. He raced to it and tried the handle.

"Donna?" he yelled, pounding on the door. "Are you in there?"

Brent opened his mouth to ask a question, when Marco picked up a chair and crashed it into the door. Bits of wood splintered everywhere, but the door didn't budge.

He didn't waste time questioning. If there was a woman in there not responding… "Is there another way in?"

"One exit door to the outside."

"On it." Brent sprinted back down the hall and out the front door, then rounded the corner of the building.

He reached what he supposed was the correct door. Locked, but there was a large window to catch the bay view. He pressed a hand to the glass and peered in. A guy with a ski mask knelt, his knee on the back of a prostrate woman. He saw only her cascade of wavy blond hair, her

hands splayed away from her body, fingers balled into terrified fists. Across the room the door vibrated as Marco attempted to force it, probably with his booted foot this time.
Despite Marco's muscles, it was going to take a while and
the woman on the floor had no time to spare.

Brent tore his eyes away from the horrifying scene and
hunted for something solid and heavy. No rocks or handy
blocks of wood. He'd do what coasties did best: improvise.

Time to do some damage.

Donna lay on the floor stomach-down, as the man in
the ski mask had directed after he'd locked the door. Her
heart thundered in her throat. He must have seen something in the window, because he eased off her for a moment to look. Instantly, she was on her feet, scanning the
room for a weapon with which to protect herself. There
was nothing in the perfectly ordered space except for the
pitcher, which she snatched up.

The intruder's mouth twisted into a smile.

Notice the details, she heard her father say. *Most wit-
nesses can't offer anything helpful to catch the offender.*

Dark eyes, Caucasian, tall. But was she going to live
to be a witness?

He stepped close and she swung the pitcher with all her
might at his head. With one hand he batted it away. It spi-
raled through the air, hit the corner of the table and broke.
He grabbed her by the arms, forcing her down into a chair.

Tears of pain trickled down her face. Terror left her
limbs thick and lifeless.

"What do you want?" she whispered.

He loomed closer, dark eyes glittering, lips inches from
hers. "You."

Fear turned to adrenaline. She twisted and writhed in
the chair, but his grip did not loosen.

"Your pops was a big-shot marine-turned-investigator," the man said. "Are you a private eye, too?"

She shook her head, teeth clenched together.

He tangled his fingers through her hair. "That's right. You're not a detective." Leaning close, he spoke into her ear. "You're just a scared little girl."

Each word shot through her, his hot breath searing her temple.

He pulled a knife from his belt. He was going to kill her.

Again she struggled, striking out at his chest, clawing at his face, pulling at the ski mask until he jerked out of reach.

He smiled, teeth harsh white against a tangle of facial hair, the hint of beard. "I guess you think you're tough, don't you?" He wrapped a strong hand around her throat, the other grasping the knife. "Little girls who think they're tough like men. You know what happens to them?"

She tried to loosen the fingers around her throat, but he was cutting off her air.

"I said," he hissed, "do you know what happens to those little girls?"

She kicked out, missing him.

Now his mouth was pressed against her forehead and he kissed her.

Revulsion nearly made her gag. Tears stung her eyes, but she would not let him see her completely lose it.

"Those little girls…" he whispered in a tender sing-song voice, "die."

Brent saw the guy pull a knife just before he found what he was looking for, a small stone bench. Not more than a stool, really, but heavy.

He pulled it from the shrubbery, heaved it above his head and hurled it into the window. It shattered with a crash. He dragged it in a circular motion to swipe away the glass. Then he was up and over, clearing the threshold just as Marco smashed through the opposite door.

The man looked from Brent to Marco and made his decision. He went for the door.

Brent pursued. He managed to grab some of the guy's black sweat jacket, just enough to knock him off-balance. He stumbled, but he did not go down.

Brent lunged for him again, but the guy surged forward, tackling Marco, who went over on his back. The assailant rushed by and clattered down the hall. In seconds, Marco was on his feet and chasing after him.

Should he follow or stay? It wasn't even a contest. Brent's heart was always with the victim. He turned back to the woman. Her thick lashes framed wide eyes, so blue, so vibrant. He flashed on Carrie, long dead, his fault. *Knock it off, Brent.*

"Are you—?" he began.

He didn't finish the thought before she picked up a glass shard from the pitcher, wielding it like a knife.

"Get away," she said breathlessly, face wild with fear. "Don't touch me."

He held up his hands, palms out. Panic could be as dangerous as any emotion—he knew from having rescued many people on the brink of drowning. Rational thought always took a backseat to the primal need for self-preservation. Many times he'd had to physically subdue a victim in order to save both their lives. The thought rippled across his mind before he could stop it. Had Carrie felt panic in those last few moments before she drowned? With an effort, he blinked the thought away. He kept his tone light, reassuring. "It's okay. He's gone. I'm not going to hurt you."

Her skin was dead pale except for two spots of color that appeared on each cheek. "Get away." Drops of blood dripped from her palm where a glass shard was cutting into her skin.

He stayed still, hands where she could see them. "My name is Brent. I work for the coast guard." He pointed to her hand. "You're bleeding. Why don't you let me help you with that?"

She blinked, still gripping the glass. Slowly she looked at her hand as if she hadn't known what was in it.

"The man…" she stammered.

He nodded. "I saw him. He ran away and he's not coming back. Marco's chasing him."

"Marco." The dazed look in her eyes subsided and he could see her body begin to tremble like a leaf in storm-tossed water.

"Why don't you sit down?" He pulled a chair out, careful not to touch her. "I'll stay here with you until Marco comes back, okay?"

She still didn't assent, but neither did she pull away when he pushed the chair toward her. Her trembling was violent now and she collapsed into it.

"I'm just going to call the police." He did so, eyeing her the whole time, checking to make sure that she was not slipping into shock.

"What's your name?" he said as he finished the call and clicked off the phone.

"Donna."

"Nice to meet you, Donna."

He took a knee and slowly, very slowly, touched her wrist with his finger. "Can you open this hand for me?"

"Are you a doctor?" she whispered.

"Rescue swimmer and an EMT. I've been known to try my hand at doctoring a time or two. I'm a whiz with bandages."

Her fingers opened like a flower and he flicked the glass away. Taking a pile of napkins from the sideboard, he pressed them to the cuts on her hand. "Squeeze, okay? Not too bad, just some shallow wounds. Probably won't even need stitches." Her fingers were elegant, long and tapering, strong. He found himself glad she would likely not bear a scar from the attack, not a physical one, anyway.

Mentally he'd been measuring the time, wondering about Marco. Shouldn't he have returned by now? Her eyes, which he now saw were true navy blue, never left his face. She was, he realized, now that the terror was ebbing slightly from her expression, lovely. Like Carrie, only not.

Sirens sounded in the distance.

"Won't be long."

"Where's Marco?" she said, only a slight tremble in her voice now.

He eyed the door. "As soon as the cops get here, I'll go find him."

She caught her full lower lip between her teeth.

"Don't worry—from what I saw, he's a big gorilla."

Marco appeared in the doorway. "The gorilla's back."

Brent's gut relaxed until he saw the ragged edge on Marco's shirt and the blood seeping into the waistband of his jeans.

Donna leaped from the chair, brushed aside Brent's restraining hands and ran to Marco. "You're bleeding."

"Minor. Did he hurt you?"

"No. Just scared me. Sit down. This man…" She looked at Brent. "He's got some medical training."

Brent raised an eyebrow. "You should do what she says. I'm certain she's smarter than you."

Marco reluctantly sat in the chair and Brent took a look at his wound. "Long and shallow."

"Minor, like I said."

Donna snatched up more napkins and handed them to

Brent, who placed them on the wound. When he tried to hold them in place, Marco swatted his hands away.

"I can do it."

"What happened?" Brent asked. "You forgot to duck?"

"Sliced me, and made it to his truck."

Donna knew she should be terrified that the crazy attacker was out there somewhere, but at the moment, she could feel only relief. Marco, a man who was like a brother to her, was not seriously hurt.

She turned to Brent. He was tall, a good six feet, with broad shoulders and the required military short haircut. Dark eyes, thick brows, an old bruise healing on his forehead. "Thank you, for what you did."

He shrugged. "No problem."

She quirked an eyebrow. "Why are you here?"

Marco huffed. "That's what I was trying to get out of him."

The police arrived then, sirens blaring. Three officers raced in, hands on their guns.

Marco filled them in.

The tallest one, a uniformed woman, introduced herself as Officer Huffington. Donna knew her even before the introduction. She'd been the one to show up in the hospital after her father was pronounced dead. Professional, unemotional. Donna felt anything but. Huffington listened intently to the three as they related the story as best they could.

"Now do you see what I've been saying? Someone was after my father. He came here trying to scare me." *And it worked*, she said to herself. Her knees were still shaking, palms ice-cold.

"We'll investigate, I can assure you, Ms. Gallagher, but what would his motive be, this guy?"

"To stop me from investigating."

"Investigating what?"

Brent edged forward. "I'd like to hear that, too."

Officer Huffington gave him the once-over. "So I guess this is the part when you tell me why you happened to be here at eleven thirty on a rainy night."

Marco grunted as a paramedic cleansed the wound.

Brent's eyes darkened, all traces of a smile gone. "I found the address to this business at my sister's apartment. I haven't heard from her recently. I was worried. I came here."

"Who is your sister?" Officer Huffington said.

Brent pointed to the name on the file sitting on the conference table.

"Pauline Mitchell. Seems like Bruce Gallagher was looking into something for my sister." He looked squarely at Donna. "I'd like to know what that was."

THREE

After a volley of questions and answers, Officer Huffington moved to speak with her officers. Brent wanted to talk to Donna, but Marco fielded most of the questions in a maddeningly brusque manner. Brent realized that Marco was trying to get rid of him. Reasonable. It was going on 12:30 a.m. The man was obviously family to Donna, and the woman had just been through a violent attack on the heels of losing Bruce Gallagher. He was sorry to have to press, but the roaring of his instincts would not be quieted now.

"My sister is missing," he stated again calmly. "She obviously went to see Bruce Gallagher on some private matter." Too private to tell her brother. He swallowed the guilt. "I want to know what it was about."

Donna looked him over, pale but resolute. "Mr. Mitchell, I know your sister. I'm a vet. She brought her dog, Radar, in to see me a month and a half ago, but I don't know what she discussed with my father. I remember chatting with her that Dad was an investigator, but I had no idea she was his client."

"What's in the file?"

She jerked her head toward the manila folder still sitting on the conference table. "Nothing, really. Just some names."

"What names?"

Officer Huffington rejoined the conversation. "What makes you think your sister is missing, Mr. Mitchell?"

"Haven't heard from her for three weeks."

"Is that unusual?"

He rolled a shoulder as a new wave of guilt hit. "No, but I've left messages that she hasn't returned."

Donna nodded. "I've repeatedly called to check on Radar, her dog, and she didn't return those calls, either."

"Any discussion about her taking a trip?"

Brent shook his head. "Not that I know of."

"Actually," Donna said, "when she brought Radar in, she mentioned a trip to Carmel."

Brent sighed inwardly. Of course she hadn't told him. He'd never made the time to listen. She did not take priority above his coast guard duties. *Be the hero to everyone but your own sister, Brent.*

"Okay," Huffington said. "Give me Pauline's address and I'll send someone over to look at her place after our search for this guy is concluded."

Brent provided the address.

She looked at Donna. "And I'll need a copy of what's in your father's file."

Donna went to the copier in the corner. He noticed she was careful to screen his view. She was protecting some sort of information because she didn't trust him. Gratitude for his catapult through her window went only so far. He suspected the Gallaghers and company were a tight-knit clan.

Fine. He'd get the information he needed one way or another, and he wasn't about to wait until the cops made time to search Pauline's home. The Mitchells could be tight-knit, too, just the two of them. "All right. I'll be going, then, if you don't need anything further."

"Got your info," Huffington said, looking up from her discussion with another officer.

Donna followed him to the front door, looking as though she was puzzling through something.

"Thank you," she blurted. "I appreciate what you did for me."

He stepped onto the porch, a patter of raindrops falling around him. "No problem. Is there a reason you don't want me to know what's in that folder?"

The lighting didn't allow him to see it, but he had the sense her face flushed a rosy red.

"There's not much, I told you."

"But there's something, and I think I have the right to know. She's my sister."

"And I think I have the right not to tell you. You're a stranger and he's…" She swallowed, a little gulp. "He was my father."

The vulnerability in that little gulp was the only thing that kept him from pressing. It spoke of irretrievable loss, a phenomenon with which he was familiar. He thought again of his fiancée, Carrie, gentle, trusting and the woman he had been unable to save. *Focus, Brent.* He would check out his sister's place again first. Then if he needed to push Donna Gallagher, he'd do it. He extended his hand, grasping her uninjured fingers, still cold to the touch, between his palms. She squeezed back for a moment before pulling away.

"Good night, Donna," he said.

He felt her eyes follow him as he walked out into the rain.

Donna's sisters arrived in short order. Younger sister Angela wrapped her in a smothering embrace. She was a good four inches taller than Donna's five-six. Donna was so grateful that Angela had been given leave from her job as navy chaplain to minister to her own family after her father's death.

Angela sat Donna down at the table and listened in that quiet way of hers. Her silence had only intensified since her return from Afghanistan. Their oldest sister, Candace, arrived halfway through the story, her mass of dark curly hair mussed and windblown. Candace's mothering instinct kicked in.

"You should go to the hospital," she said to Marco, with a frown of concern. She touched his cheek with her hand. Donna saw a flicker of tenderness flash in Marco's eyes. She wondered why Candace never seemed to see it.

He ducked his head. "Aww, I'm all right."

"Try letting someone help you for a change. Let me see how well they bandaged the wound." Candace inspected, grudgingly agreeing that the paramedic's work was passable.

"I thought you were catching a flight today, Marco," Angela said.

"I am. Red-eye."

It was a difficult time. Marco was flying to Georgia for the funeral of a woman he'd loved since he was a teen and probably always would, even though she'd died of a drug overdose. And this following on the heels of the memorial service for Bruce, the man who'd been his best friend.

Candace sighed and gave him a hug. He reached one big hand around her as if to gather her closer but didn't.

"I'm sorry," Candace said. "Please go if you need to. We all understand."

"Not until this situation is under control."

Angela helped herself to a cup of coffee. "I heard everything you said, Donna, but I see in your face that there's something more, so tell us."

"This attack wasn't random. The guy wanted something in Dad's files."

She caught the look Candace leveled at Angela. The "she's going off the deep end" look.

Angela spoke carefully. "What do the police think?"

"Their position hasn't changed. They think Dad's death was an accident."

Candace laid a hand on Donna's shoulder and squeezed.

"Honey, is it easier to think that Dad's death was intentional because then you can do something about it? Get justice for him somehow? Or maybe…"

It would help you forget the hurt you caused Dad? The way you flouted his advice and took up with the wrong guy? Donna stood abruptly. "No, that's not it. The circumstances confirm what I'm thinking. Pauline disappears. Dad dies. Someone breaks into the office. That's not coincidence."

Angela sipped from her mug. "Why did Pauline come to Dad in the first place?"

"I don't know. I wonder if she was afraid someone was after her and the names in the file are Dad's suspect list."

Marco cleared his throat. "Why didn't you tell the coastie what was in the file?"

She wanted to brush aside the question because she was afraid her answer would make her sound even crazier to her sisters, but Marco would not let her look away.

"Because Brent Mitchell's name is number one on the list."

Brent jogged back to the Glorietta Bay Marina and boarded the boat he was taking care of for a buddy. His friend's 1988 Bayliner motoryacht had seen better days. It was small, but then, so was his studio apartment near the San Diego Naval Base. He didn't particularly care where he slept so long as it was near the beach and plenty of places to run and train. Coronado would not be his first choice, since he'd learned that Dan Ridley, Carrie's ex-boyfriend, had been hired as the island's newest cop. Ridley blamed Brent for Carrie's death six years before. The guy was right. If it hadn't been for Brent, they would never have been up in that small plane in the first place.

"I don't like flying," Carrie had said. "And it's stormy today."

He'd embraced her. He was a brash twenty-two-year-old new coast guard seaman who wasn't afraid of anything in the world. "I'll be right there in case something happens, but it won't. Planes are safer than cars," he'd teased.

Only this Cessna 152 hadn't been, and a perfect day of whale watching had turned into the worst day of his life when the engine failed and the plane slammed into the Pacific Ocean. The sound of Carrie's screams and the pilot's frantic Mayday still echoed in his ears after six long years. Both had died on impact. Brent, for some reason that he could not fathom, had not. Brent pressed down the throbbing in his gut, threw on some dry clothes and hopped on his motorcycle, grateful that the rain had slowed to a mist.

As he drove to his sister's home not far from Coronado Beach, his thoughts thrummed through him with growing urgency.

Where is she? And what had Donna's father known about it?

He tried to keep his thoughts positive without success. Being the sole survivor of a plane crash tended to strip the optimism out of a person. He struggled with the tragedy, and the God who allowed it, every moment of his life. And every rescue mission he went on, every time he geared up and strapped into that helicopter, he resolved to defeat the ocean and God in order to get that victim out alive. Most of the time, he won. Sometimes not. This time, he was not about to lose.

He parked the bike in the driveway of Pauline's quaint Tudor home. White icicle lights decorated the eaves, reflecting sparks on the rain-soaked grass. Up and down the block, strings of lights gave the houses a holiday glow and he thought of his sister's enthusiasm for Christmas. Pauline insisted on putting out her festive decor the day after Thanksgiving and went so far as to burgle his apartment one year to install a tree on his kitchen table, complete with tinsel and popcorn strings and some creepy elf thing.

"You're a grinch, Brent," she'd said. "The holiday is supposed to be filled with rejoicing."

Rejoicing wasn't something he'd ever made time for. Fun, sometimes. Mischief, certainly. But now he wondered if he'd missed the mark. Lives were so fragile, blown out in a moment like a candle in a strong wind. His heart thumped hard.

Quit going to the worst-case scenario. You're going to find her.

He upended the stone rabbit sculpture where Pauline had always hidden a spare key and where he'd replaced it after his visit last week.

Pausing before he fitted the key into the lock, he noted a car driving slowly by. He stepped into the shadows. It was not the vehicle he'd seen at the Gallagher place. The vehicle continued on. He waited. Another three minutes and it came by again, this time, pulling to a stop.

A familiar figure got out.

"Busy night for you," he said.

Donna jumped. "You scared me."

"That's because you're the trespasser now. I'm surprised Marco let you come here alone." Even in the dim light, he could see the chagrin on her face.

"He's traveling," she mumbled.

"And you waited until after he left, didn't you?"

She flipped her hair away from her cheeks, her posture straight, defiant. "I need to know."

Brent noted how her skin shone luminous in the moonlight. "Thought you were a veterinarian. Decided to take up the family business?"

She stiffened. "Shouldn't we take a look inside?"

Brent considered. "We? I didn't think you were interested in working together on this."

She stayed quiet for a moment. "Figuring out what happened to Pauline may shed some light on why my father was murdered. We're both after the same thing."

"All right," he said. "Let's go inside, then. I've already checked it out, but maybe I missed something."

Donna considered the house. "This is a nice place. What does your sister do for a living?"

"She's the activities director for a group home for mentally challenged adults."

He read the expression, the one that said, "And how does someone who makes that kind of money afford a house like this in Coronado?" "She was married, briefly. Her husband died. She bought this house with the life insurance money." *Not that it's any of your business*, he felt like adding.

They entered the kitchen and Brent turned on the lights. Spotless. It was always spotless, even during his last visit on Thanksgiving, when they'd eaten take-out chow mein after she'd burned the turkey and they'd watched an old Abbott and Costello movie. Everything was painted in soothing ivory, complementing the marbled counters. Fat red Christmas candles sat on the kitchen table, unburned.

Just like last time, he saw nothing unusual, until he noticed the corner of a plastic bag sticking out from the kitchen drawer. Inside, he found a plastic zip-top bag containing travel bottles of shampoo, conditioner and hand lotion. A Post-it note was stuck to the bag. *Stop mail.*

His heart surged as he held it up for Donna to see. Pauline really was on a trip. He wondered why he hadn't noticed the bag sticking out of the drawer on his last visit.

"Everything looks neat and tidy," Donna said. She opened the refrigerator. For some reason, the intrusion into Pauline's privacy bothered Brent. "There's nothing left to spoil. That seems to confirm she's traveling. Her car's not here, either. What does she drive?"

"Old orange Toyota. I tell her she looks like she's driving a pumpkin, but she loves the color."

"Where's Radar?" Donna pointed to an empty food bowl next to a nearly dry water dish.

"Pauline never leaves Radar behind. If she's on a trip, she's probably taken him along," Brent said.

"Or she might have boarded him in a kennel," Donna said. "I can check into that."

The kitchen phone rang, jarring in the silence of the house.

Brent picked it up, recognizing the number, the same caller who had contacted his cell earlier. "Who is this?" He put the phone on speaker.

"I want to know where she left it." High voice, shaky, nervous.

"What? Who is this?"

There was a muffled sob. "I told her he was dangerous."

Brent found himself holding his breath. "Who is this and what do you know about my sister?"

"I've gotta get out of here." The man's voice dissolved into more crying.

"Stay on the line," Brent commanded, his skin prickling. "Tell me what you know about my sister."

But the caller had hung up.

Donna's lips were pressed together in a thin line. "That number," she said, pointing to the number on the phone's tiny digital screen. "It's not the same person who called the office."

"Was it the voice of the man who attacked you?"

"I can't say for sure. I don't think so."

Two guys?

He stared at the phone, jaw tight.

"Did you hear that?" Donna cocked her head, and he noticed for the first time that her long hair was spangled with raindrops.

He listened. A slow scraping sound teased his skin into goose bumps.

"Where's that coming from?" he murmured.

"Below," she whispered, looking to the narrow staircase in the corner of the kitchen. "There's someone down there."

He heard it then, a long slow movement, the sound of someone dragging a dead weight.

In the basement.

FOUR

Donna tensed as Brent started for the stairs at a sprint. "Wait here," he said.

"Not likely."

He flashed her a roguish smile that made her want to smile back and then eased open the door. The stairwell was dark. She listened, her hand finding his back, reading the tension coiled in his shoulders.

"Is this the only way in and out?" she whispered, catching the fragrance of his aftershave.

"Two basement windows," he answered. "They open onto the backyard. A small bathroom window, too." Below them, the sweep of a flashlight beam cut unsteadily through the darkness.

He paused, fingers on the light switch. "Here we go," he whispered. Snapping on the light, he hurtled down the stairs.

Donna figured they had the advantage. Their eyes were already adjusted to the light. She heard a crash as they emerged into the paneled space, boxes arranged into neat stacks that reached the low ceiling. In the dim light she made out a small table covered with balls of yarn. Three bags of dog kibble were piled nearby. The room was dim. A door slammed.

"Come out of there," Brent shouted.

It took her a moment to realize the intruder had rushed into the tiny bathroom. Brent was at the bathroom door in a moment. Finding it locked, he kicked at it. The cheap wood began to give way almost immediately.

Donna looked around for something to use as a weapon. Broom? Tennis racket? She found nothing until she noticed a small hatchet next to a neatly stacked pile of wood. She snatched it up, the cold metal seeming to leach into her nerves, freezing her fingertips. The door splintered with a shriek of the metal hinges under Brent's feet. From inside the bathroom came the sound of glass exploding.

Without a breath of warning, the noises catapulted her back to the memory of her own accident, flying off the seat of Nate's motorcycle, a vehicle her father had forbidden her to ride with a man whom he had tried his utmost to warn her about. He'd been right, she'd realized when she'd woken up temporarily paralyzed with Nate nowhere to be found. Bruce Gallagher had been dead-on correct, and she'd raged at him for it.

Swallowing the guilt, she regripped the hatchet to rally her senses just as the door failed. Brent shoved it open.

They stumbled through in time to see a pair of legs disappearing through the small window above the toilet. Brent grabbed at the feet, a moment too late. One shoe made contact, smashing him in the cheek, sending him stumbling.

Donna was already racing back up the steps by the time Brent recovered and followed. They sprinted through the house and out into the backyard. Donna almost tumbled into the pool. Brent snatched at her T-shirt as she teetered on the edge, pulling her tight against his chest for a moment.

She felt his heart hammering, or was it her own? "Thanks," she whispered, pulling away.

Skirting the water, they made it to the short stuccoed retaining wall that enclosed the yard, fringed with delicate flowers and shrubbery.

On the other side of the wall was a smooth paved path that led down to the beach in one direction and back to the main road in the other. The moon showed silver white on the pavement.

No movement. No sound except the waves.

Brent jogged toward the beach until she lost sight of him. She made her way cautiously in the other direction, ears straining for any sign, any sound. Nothing. She scanned the thick shrubbery that lined the road, part of the charm and ambiance of Coronado Island.

Was the intruder hiding somewhere? Watching? Was it the same man who had held a knife to her throat at the office? Shivers erupted through her body and she wished she had stayed put. She realized she was gripping the hatchet so tight her fingers were cramping. A few more paces and something crackled in the branches. Shivers surged up her spine.

"Come out," she ordered, forcing the words. Every muscle in her body tensed. What if he did emerge? Would she really have the fortitude to use a hatchet to defend herself?

Her lungs wouldn't work properly; blood pounded in her temples. She caught a glimpse, the quickest flash of a feline face regarding her, before the cat retreated back into the bushes.

"Nice work, Donna," she muttered to herself. "Way to scare off a cat."

Running feet made her breath catch. Brent jogged up to her.

"Anything?" she said.

"No. Whoever it was, I give them points for speed. And I thought my eight-minute time on the mile-and-a-half run was good." He shook his head. "Not good enough." He eyed her hands. "Hatchet?"

"There wasn't a stun gun handy."

He smiled, but now it was strained, pinched around the edges with worry.

"Let's go look in the basement and see if we can figure out what the guy was after," she said.

He raised an eyebrow. "Maybe you really are a detective."

"Don't make fun of me," she snapped. "I never said I was anything but a vet."

"I wasn't making fun."

"Yes, you were."

He held up his palms and let out a low breath. "Sometimes I try too hard to be witty and it just comes out like I'm a smart aleck. I'm sorry. Character flaw."

There was an earnestness in his tone that quenched her fire. "It's okay. Sometimes I take offense when I shouldn't. My character flaw."

"Truce, then."

She allowed him to take her hand and help her back over the stucco wall. His fingers were strong and warm. It had been a long time since she'd held a man's hand, and the touch reassured her. But she didn't need reassurance, not from a man, not now. With the memory of Nate threatening to surface, she pulled away and tried to focus her thoughts.

What was she hoping to find in the basement? Her father would know. Grief welled afresh in her heart. *You don't have to be a detective*, she chided herself. *You just have to be observant and you've had plenty of training for that.* With canine clients, she'd learned to watch every detail, every nuance of their behavior, to ferret out answers. She'd do the same in this situation.

Her foot clunked against something hard as she walked through the darkened yard. She stopped to check.

"Brent?"

He was almost to the door. "Yeah?"

Her mind knew what she was seeing, but somehow she could not make sense of it. "I think you'd better come take a look at this."

Brent stared at the small suitcase. He knew every crack and scrape on the old leather. It was his father's. Before he died of liver cancer when they were in grade school, they'd seen him pack and unpack that case hundreds of times. Neat, precise, deliberate, right down to the socks nestled inside his extra pair of shoes. Brent packed the same way.

"Daddy has to go where the bridges are," his mother would say of her construction foreman husband.

Pauline used to cry. Every time. Brent couldn't see the sense in the tears. His mother said God would bring Roger Mitchell back safely, and Brent had trusted in that. Turned out that God took their father a different way, through the tumors that ate up his liver. The disease had taken his mother, too, when Pauline and his sister were nearly through high school. Not cancer, but the lonely silence of an empty house that abraded her will to live. God wasn't enough to fill that void. He wasn't enough to fill Brent's, either.

He realized Donna was speaking.

"We shouldn't touch it. I've called the police."

No more waiting. Pauline was in trouble, he could feel it. He bent down and shone his cell phone light onto the case. Using the edge of his shirt to touch the clasps, he opened it.

"Brent…" Donna started.

He ignored her.

The case opened and they looked inside. Pauline's pajamas, fuzzy purple, her slippers, hairbrush, jeans, a T-shirt.

"What is going on here?" he heard Donna murmur.

All he could do was stare into the suitcase. His sister's things. What possible explanation could there be?

"Brent," she said again. "You don't think the person we were chasing was your sister, do you?"

He stood, trying to remember the size of the feet he'd almost grabbed as they disappeared out the window. "It couldn't have been."

"Aren't these her things?"

"Yes, but it wasn't her," he repeated.

"How do you know?"

"Because," he fired off, "she wouldn't have run from me."

Donna stared at him with what looked like a mixture of pity and disbelief. He tried for a softer voice, an apologetic smile.

"Pauline and I are close. If she was in trouble, she would come to me."

"Maybe she didn't know it was you in the basement."

"Maybe." He looked doubtfully at the suitcase. Pauline was running? From him? So scared she'd jumped out a basement window? Why hadn't she called him? Texted? His hands went clammy as he stowed the cell phone. "It must not have been her."

"But who else would take these things? They're of no value to anyone but your sister."

He didn't have an answer. Nothing seemed to rise above the feeling of dread that settled into his gut. A police car rolled up with lights but no sirens. Donna went to greet it. Brent stayed with the suitcase. For some reason, he did not want it left alone in the darkened yard. A thought lifted his spirit. If it was really Pauline he'd been chasing, it confirmed she was alive and that was good enough at the moment. A glimmer of hope from God, his mother would say. The feeling didn't last long. There was no hope from God, he'd learned, only loss and bitter despair.

"What are the chances?" a low voice said.

Brent looked up to see the man who hated him more than any other human being on the planet staring at him through the mist. Officer Dan Ridley. Brent's heart sank. He forced an even tone.

"My sister's in trouble."

Ridley rested his hands on his gun belt. He looked tired, his mouth pulled down into a grimace. "Lots of women around you get in trouble."

Brent saw Donna's questioning look.

Ridley glanced at her. "She doesn't know?"

"Where's Officer Huffington?" Brent spat.

"She had to fly to Los Angeles to testify in court. This is my beat now." Ridley smiled. "So you've got a problem, huh? Imagine how sorry I am to hear it."

"Can we cut the sarcasm?" Brent's pulse slammed against his throat.

Ridley introduced himself to Donna. "I guess you and this guy must be new friends, or else you would know."

There was the slightest unpleasant inflection on the word *friends*.

"Know what?" Donna said.

Ridley answered before Brent could step in. "He talked a young woman into going on a flight she didn't want to take and the plane went down. Everyone died, except for the miracle man here." Ridley stared at Brent. "The sole survivor. Imagine that."

He didn't have to imagine. He woke in the middle of the night sweating, grateful to be snapped from the nightmare only to find he was never free of it and never would be.

"It's good to be a strong swimmer," Ridley said. "You took off for shore in a heartbeat, I imagine. Didn't even stop to help your dying fiancée, did you?"

Donna recoiled in disgust. "This isn't the time or place."

"I'm sure Mitchell here would agree with you. It's never the time or the place to admit that you cost someone their life."

"That's enough," Donna snapped.

Brent couldn't stand her defending him. It took everything in him to keep his fists at his sides. "This isn't about her dying—it's about her leaving. Carrie dumped you, Dan, and chose me. That hurts you more than her death, doesn't it? What kind of a guy does that make you?"

Ridley jerked forward.

Donna stepped between them. "Can we focus on what's happened right here?" She gestured to the suitcase. "Whatever past you two have going on, there's a woman in danger right now. Is there another officer who can help us now, since you're not able to be professional?"

Ridley's nostrils flared.

Brent gritted his teeth and waited.

Ridley shot Donna a hostile look before he stepped back. He called to another officer, who approached, camera in hand, taking pictures of the suitcase. "Sergeant Cook is here to document, but I'm the lead. I'm going to walk the house with Cook and we'll photograph," Ridley said. "Then you can tell me everything from the beginning."

Inwardly, Brent groaned as the two officers headed for the house. He didn't want to consider how Donna had perceived Ridley's attack. He should explain it, tell her his side, but he could not open that dark place, not now, with a woman he barely knew.

Donna did not press. They waited in silence until Cook called them back into the house and they returned to the basement to go through the story again.

"And you don't know if the person you tried to stop is your sister?" Ridley asked.

Brent's face warmed. "All I saw were the feet."

"There's no sign of forced entry, which indicates somebody had a key. The big question is, if it was your sister, why would she run from you?" Ridley's eyes glinted and the curve of his lip told Brent the guy was enjoying every moment.

"I want another cop to investigate."

"It's a small town and there aren't any others available, so you're stuck with me until Huffington returns. Ironic, isn't it?"

Brent raged. "I'll talk to the chief."

"Go ahead, but you'll still be working with me. We'll

start the ball rolling and come back tomorrow to see if we missed anything." His satisfied smile lasted a moment longer before it dimmed. "Look, I wouldn't cross the street for you, Mitchell, but I'm good at my job and I'll do my best for your sister, if she really is in trouble." He headed for the basement stairs. "Goodness knows Pauline doesn't deserve to suffer like Carrie did."

The officers trailed up the basement steps and departed, leaving Brent staring at a closed door, even more confused than he'd been twelve hours before. One thing was certain, Pauline was in trouble. Big-time.

In Pauline's basement, Donna trailed her fingers through the pile of yarn, uncertain whether to stay or go. She itched to talk over the developments with Marco and her sisters, but Brent's unnatural stillness kept her there. Ridley's hateful accusations circled in her mind and left her angry. Whatever had happened in their past, Pauline's safety should be the focus and Brent was right to ask for a new investigator to take charge. Unless…

The suspicion wormed its way to the surface. What if Brent was not as innocent as he seemed? The handsome face, the little-boy vulnerability—she'd been fooled before.

To cover her confusion, she made a pretense of examining the knitting supplies. The yarns were in hues of greens and blues, next to what appeared to be the beginnings of a crooked scarf. Donna's mother, JeanBeth, was a skilled knitter and it was easy to see that Pauline was not. Brent remained locked in silence. The minutes ticked away. She'd just decided to go when he spoke.

"She makes me a scarf every year for Christmas. Sews me vests, too."

She remained silent, willing him to continue. For some reason that she could not name, she wanted to know what was going on inside Brent Mitchell.

"I don't wear scarves, living in Southern California, but I put them on to please her. I've got five hanging in my closet. Five scarves. Some of them have holes in them and she says those are 'in the French style.'" He smiled. "I tell her I like them better that way because it allows for ventilation. The vests are even worse. It's ironic because rescue swimmers sew their own gear, so I can handle a needle and thread better than she does. I never tell her that."

"You're a good brother."

His eyes found hers. "I wish that was true. Since the plane crash…" He cleared his throat. "You're probably wondering about all that since Ridley dropped the bomb."

"You were the only survivor?"

"Yes." He looked away, eyes studying the ceiling. "For the last six years since it happened, I've immersed myself in work. I've been so busy that I didn't make enough time for my sister."

Donna sighed. "I've used that trick myself, hiding at work."

He sank down on a wooden trunk. "Yeah? Seems like you have everything squared away with your family. Close with the sisters, Marco."

"Let's just say I had plenty of excuses not to hear the truth that my father and Marco were trying to deliver." She sighed. "I'm working on getting rid of that guilt."

"I didn't think it was possible, letting go of guilt."

She considered his troubled face. "It's not easy, that's for sure."

He looked as though he wanted to ask a question. Instead, he stood up. "Getting late."

"Yes."

"I'll walk you to your car."

"No need."

"I know. Gonna do it, anyway."

He put a hand on her shoulder to guide her to the steps

and it made her pulse quicken. "Her work," Donna blurted out. "That's the next place to look."

He fastened those rich brown eyes on hers, making something tingle inside. "I'm sure the police will check out the group home. It's a place called Open Vistas. See if they can glean anything. That's where I'm headed tomorrow, too. Ridley will be thrilled to see me again."

She was sorry when his hand fell away.

They walked out into the front yard. The house looked peaceful in the moonlight, a picture of tranquility and comfort, the whole street bathed in Christmas cheer. Until Pauline was found, there would be no celebration in his life.

"I'm on your father's list, aren't I?" he said as he opened her car door for her and she climbed in.

"I don't know what you mean."

"Yes, you do. My sister went to your dad because she was afraid of someone. When she stopped coming around, your father started doing some informal checking and, being the thorough investigator type, he jotted me down there on the suspect list."

She winced.

He thrummed his fingers on the roof of the car. "Why wouldn't I be a suspect? I'm the beneficiary of her life insurance policy, I think. A natural conclusion. I could have been plotting to murder her or something." He laughed, bitter and low. "Ridley would love to consider me a suspect in my own sister's disappearance."

His hands were on his hips now, jaw drawn tight.

"I don't know what my father was investigating," she said honestly. "I wish I did."

"For what it's worth, I love my sister. She's the only person on this earth who knows what a jerk I can be and loves me, anyway. I did not hurt her. I never would."

The far-off sound of the waves filled in the silence.

His eyes searched her face. "Do you believe me?"

Did she? She'd believed Nate so completely, surrendering her common sense, going along to parties, excusing his drinking and his job hopping, believing every lie he'd told her. But God had saved her and He and her father had never stopped loving her or trusting in her, even when she so richly had deserved it. Did she believe Brent? A man she hardly knew? A man Ridley blamed for a young woman's death?

Mist beaded on his hair and she saw in the creases under his eyes, the tightening in his lips, that Brent Mitchell was a man in anguish. "Yes," she found herself saying. "I do believe you."

His mouth opened as if he meant to speak. Instead, he sighed, long and slow, a whoosh of air that mingled with the murmur of the waves against the sand. "Thank you for that," he said.

The moonlight glimmered between them, painting dark streaks across his face.

"I'd better go," she said. As she drove off, she sneaked a look in the rearview. He stayed there, hands shoved into his pockets, watching her depart.

She drove slowly along the darkened street. Everywhere, the shadows were thick, impenetrable. A million tiny movements, probably nothing more than the wind on the leaves, made her stomach tighten. Was someone watching her progress? The same man who had held a knife to her throat?

She double-checked that she'd locked the car doors.

"Your fear is running away with you. There's no threat out there in the night," she told herself, out loud for emphasis.

Still, she made sure she'd pulled the car in the garage and waited until the door closed before she unlocked the car and scurried into the house.

FIVE

Nightmares trickled through Donna's sleep, forcing her awake before the sun rose. Groggy and lethargic, she put herself through her Pilates exercises until her stiff muscles finally cooperated. Since the accident that had broken her back and temporarily paralyzed her, pain was a constant companion and no doubt a lifelong one, but Donna was determined to beat it back to a manageable level. She had a quick temper, but she'd begun to funnel her anger into her exercise. "Defeat the pain every day," her father had said.

Her eyes flicked to the closet where her wheelchair was stowed, a reminder of how she'd once given up completely in the face of her paralysis. She'd surrendered her will and her future to hopelessness, shoving away everyone who loved her and the God she imagined did not. Dark times that she would not revisit. A knock at the door startled her. Remembering the skin-crawling sensation of being watched from the night before, she crept to the door on tiptoe.

One glance through the peephole and she knew she was in trouble. Two very determined sisters stood on her doorstep at six fifteen on a Thursday morning, and Angela was holding a white bag. Gallagher-sister determination plus doughnuts was a powerful combination.

Meekly, she opened the door. "Isn't it a little early?"

Candace thrust a cup of coffee into her hand. "Only for someone who has been out late at night."

She flinched. "How did you find out?"

"Coronado is a small town. Marcy Owens lives across the street from Pauline's place. She saw you there and texted me. So why exactly were you prowling around strange houses where there may or may not have been a crime committed?"

"Alone," Angela added, sitting on the sofa and fishing out an old-fashioned glazed doughnut that she offered to Donna. "Don't forget that she was all alone."

Donna sighed and took the sweet. "Okay. It wasn't smart."

"Dad would have said you were shooting high and right," Angela said.

The old marine term struck at her. A reminder of the military life they shared with their father but she did not. "Don't speak for Dad. He's not here, remember?" She was shocked at her own outburst.

Angela's mouth tightened. "We both remember, just as well as you."

"I'm sorry," Donna said, sinking onto the old cane-backed rocker across from Angela. "I don't know where that came from."

Angela leaned forward. "You're grieving. It's okay. We are, too."

But she wanted to say, *You didn't break Dad's heart, did you?* Angela, the proud navy chaplain; Candace, married to a marine whom Bruce had adored and mother to Tracy, who'd lit up Bruce's life like no one else. Sarah, the spunky, determined surgical nurse. And then there was Donna, who'd gone off the deep end two years ago and nearly thrown her life away for a manipulating jerk. Past history. Not important, she told herself, but her guilt whispered otherwise.

She put the doughnut on the coffee table, appetite gone. "I'm not acting out of grief. Dad was murdered and I want to find out who is responsible."

She'd meant the words to shock and they had. Candace gathered her mass of curly hair and shoved it behind her ears. "If that's the case," she said slowly, "then the police will do their jobs. It's not a good idea for you to get mixed up in their business."

"There's a problem with the police. Dad's case is linked to Pauline's and the cop who's in charge now that Officer Huffington's been called away hates Brent Mitchell. I'm not sure he's going to give the case his best,"

Angela lifted an eyebrow. "Brent? The guy who was in the office when you were attacked?"

She nodded.

"If the police are hostile to Brent, and he was on the list in Dad's file…" Angela said.

"Then you need to stay away from him," Candace finished.

"Because you think I'm going to get involved with the wrong guy again, just like I did with Nate?"

"No, Donna," Angela said. "That was a mistake. You've paid for it, you've been forgiven for it. The only person who doesn't believe that is you."

"It's always been so easy for you to accept things."

Angela's green eyes caught hers. "If you only knew," she said quietly.

Shame licked at Donna's insides as she searched her sister's face, grown so thin, so tired, since her return stateside. They suspected Angela was suffering from PTSD, but she refused to discuss it. Donna knew that for all her reluctance to talk, Angela had not left the horrors of war behind. She caught her sister's fingers. "I'm sorry. It seems like I just apologize over and over now."

Angela clasped her hand tight. "It's a tough time for the Gallaghers. We need to support each other."

"That means you shouldn't go off on some sort of detective mission by yourself," Candace put in. She tucked her small frame onto a chair, cross-legged. "You've got a veterinary practice to run—stick to that."

Candace was always the direct one; tactless, some might

say, but since she'd lost Rick in Afghanistan five years before, she'd been softened and tempered. It shone on her face, through the bossiness. Inside, she was tender, fragile as spun glass. Still, they did their share of battling.

"I've closed my practice for a week."

Candace frowned. "Maybe too much free time isn't a good idea right now."

"Don't tell me how to deal with this, Candace."

Her eyes flashed. "I've had some experience with loss that you haven't."

"I understand that." She resented her sister for telling her how she should grieve. "How's Sarah?" she said to change the subject. "I didn't get a text yet this morning. Any progress?"

"Stable, but they're keeping her in the coma for another few days until the brain swelling goes down," Angela said.

"How's the blood pressure?"

"Meds are holding it to an appropriate level." Angela sighed. "Ironic."

It was ironic because Sarah, a surgical nurse, would not even take an aspirin unless she was in dire straits.

There's poison in every pill, she'd say.

And their father's death was the bitterest pill of all.

"Don't stray from the point," Candace said before finishing her doughnut. "Please tell us that you're done with the sleuthing. My nerves can't take much more."

"I am going to visit Open Vistas today. That's where Pauline Mitchell worked."

Candace stood and began to pace. "What do you hope to find out there?"

"I don't know." Brent's haggard face surfaced in her mind. Was she looking for a reason to see him? She could not be that ridiculous. "But I've got to do it."

"Can't you wait until Marco's back? If he heard about this…" Candace started.

"Don't tell him. The man needs to grieve. It isn't fair to have him worrying about things back home."

"Agreed," Angela said. "But you've got to promise that it ends after your visit to Open Vistas."

Candace gaped at Angela. "Don't tell me you think it's a good idea for her to get involved in this?"

"It's not, but I also don't think she can get into too much trouble at an assisted living facility." She offered a rueful glance over the top of her coffee cup as she sipped. "Besides, I think that when she arrives, the police are going to tell her to get lost in no uncertain terms."

"And she's going to listen to them better than she does to us?"

Angela shrugged. "They've got badges and guns. We've got doughnuts and coffee."

Donna laughed, grateful that God had blessed her with these nosy, maddening sisters. "I promise I'm going to stay out of trouble."

"Uh-huh." Candace remained unconvinced. "When are you going? I'll come along."

"Today. Soon as I can."

"Oh, man. I've got to get Tracy to school. Mom's with her right now before she goes to the hospital."

Donna felt secretly relieved.

"And I'm visiting a soldier's family today." A shadow darkened Angela's face and Donna marveled again at her sister's strength. How much sorrow had she taken on her slim shoulders, offering God's comfort to families in their darkest hour when they'd learned their soldiers were not coming home? And how could she comfort when her own soul was torn in two?

"I thought you were on leave for a while."

Angela shrugged. "They asked for me."

"No problem," Donna said. "Let's meet up this afternoon at the hospital and try to get Mom to eat something."

"Okay." Candace fixed her with a mom look of her own. "But remember that you promised to stay out of trouble. Leave the investigating to the cops."

Donna nodded meekly and accepted hugs and kisses from her sisters.

When the door closed behind them, she watched the two make their way to Candace's beloved Volvo.

Leave the investigating to the cops. You're grieving. We are, too.

You need to stay away from him.

Good reasons, sound logic, common sense.

And in spite of all of it, she grabbed her car keys and headed out.

Brent arrived at Open Vistas feeling thoroughly ashamed that he'd never visited Pauline's place of work before. He'd heard her speak of the clients, her little band of special-needs adults whom she escorted on various excursions. She loved them, especially one by the name of Harvey.

The driveway led to a tidy whitewashed building with neatly tended hibiscus shrubs flanking the path. Meandering walkways cut through the property, leading to three modern structures that appeared to be two-story apartment buildings. In his mind, he'd pictured a dormitory-style place crowded with residents. This was anything but.

He let himself into the office and met a tall man with a lush mustache and a shining bald scalp. The space was decorated with pine garlands. Elvis crooned about being home for Christmas.

Brent felt an emotional punch to the gut. Christmastime. He'd lost Carrie on December 23. Would he add his sister to the season of loss? He drove away the thought and accepted the manager's handshake.

"Welcome. I'm Kevin Carpenter. How can I help you?"

"My name's Brent Mitchell. My sister works here."

He gasped. "You're Pauline's brother?"

He nodded.

The man beamed. "Great to meet you. She's the most wonderful recreation specialist we've ever had. The residents can't wait until she returns." He shifted. "Actually, her message on the machine was unclear. Do you happen to know when she'll be back?"

"No." His stomach tightened. "When did she leave a message?"

His look grew suddenly wary. "Oh. I figured she might have shared that with you. Actually, I'm not sure I should talk about Pauline's private business. I told the other man who asked. We try to keep everything professional around here."

"What other man?"

"Private detective, name of Bruce Gallagher. I told him she was on vacation and he could talk to her when she returned. Figured he was mixed up, looking for another person maybe."

No, and now Brent knew he was also on the right trail. "I'm worried about my sister. I haven't heard from her in three weeks. The police are likely going to come and ask you the same questions I am."

His eyebrows shot up in alarm. "Police? I'm sure she's just extended her trip. It was supposed to be a few weeks. She promised she'd be back to lead the Christmas excursion to the Del."

A few more weeks of vacation and she'd show up? Brent couldn't bring himself to believe it, as much as he wanted to. And if it had been her in the basement, how could she stay on the run for that long? And why?

"Something is wrong, Mr. Carpenter. Please tell me what you know. When did she call?"

He pulled at his mustache. "It was a weekend, around

Thanksgiving. She left a phone message that she was planning a trip. It seemed abrupt. Her voice was stuffy, like she had a bad cold. I was surprised she didn't talk to me face-to-face, but she had plenty of vacation time coming. She promised she'd be back by the Christmas excursion, but I kind of expected her to show up anytime. She's never been one to stay away from Open Vistas. Always brimming with energy, that girl, and she honestly loves her work here, I'm sure of it. She and Radar are permanent fixtures even when she's not on duty."

Brent heard the throb of an approaching car. A squad car pulled onto the main road. Brent had no desire to run into Ridley again.

"Here's my number," he said, sliding a card across the counter. "Call me if you think of anything that might help find her, okay?"

"Sure. We all love Pauline. I'm going to pray that nothing has happened to her."

Wasted effort, Brent thought. Prayers were easily ignored, in his experience. He nodded. "Okay if I look around?"

Kevin handed him a name badge. "Sure, but don't bother any of our residents. This is their home."

Brent let himself out and took the nearest path under the spreading pine canopy. Fortunately, Ridley had stopped to answer his phone before going inside the office, so Brent was spared that encounter.

A group of people ranging in age from early twenties to much older sat at a picnic table. A staff member wearing the white Open Vistas T-shirt led them in some sort of book discussion. He walked on to the farthest building in the rear. Wreaths hung on most doors and some had twinkle lights outlining them.

A man with thinning hair and wire-rimmed glasses sat

on the porch, examining a calendar. He traced the numbers with a felt tipped pen over and over.

Brent did not want to startle the man, who looked up abruptly from his work. "It's Thursday, isn't it?" he asked.

"Yes," Brent said. "It's Thursday."

The man traced the numbers on his calendar. "Almost Christmas."

"Oh, yes. That's right. Are you looking forward to Christmas?"

"I'm going to the Hotel Del." He blinked, eyes magnified by the thick lenses. "Miss Pauline is taking me. We get hot cocoa and watch the fireworks."

Brent's heart sped up. "I'm Miss Pauline's brother."

He squinted at Brent, took off his glasses and polished them with a handkerchief from his pocket and put them on again. "I'm Harvey."

Harvey, the resident his sister spoke of so often. "Harvey, I've been looking for Pauline."

"She's on a trip," Harvey said.

"Did she tell you where she was going?"

"No. That's what Mr. Carpenter said."

Dead end.

"She'll come back. For Christmas. So we can go to the Del."

"I hope so, Harvey."

"She will. She left her—" He broke off suddenly, mouth closed tight, tracing the numbers with precision.

"She left what?" Brent asked.

"Nothing."

He kept his tone patient, soothing. "Harvey, did Pauline leave something with you? A note, maybe, or a phone number?"

He shook his head.

"Are you sure? It's real important that I find her."

The head shake was more agitated this time, so Brent backed off. "Okay. Thanks for talking to me, Harvey."

Harvey remained on the porch, tracing over the numbers on his calendar. Brent gritted his teeth. What had he learned? Not one single thing except that Pauline had promised this gentleman she would be there to take him to the Coronado Holiday Festival. She would never break that promise.

Unless it was not in her power to keep it.

He decided to go back to the office and face the music with the police and see if they had learned anything. Before he made it back to the main road, he got a glimpse of Donna jogging over the grass.

His blood pounded, probably just from the purposefulness in her movement. When she caught sight of him, she skidded on the wet turf, sliding to a stop at his feet.

"I'll keep my witty comments to myself," he said. "What are you doing here?"

"Come on," she said, grabbing his wrist. "You're not going to believe this."

SIX

Brent allowed himself to be towed along. Her hands were soft and smooth and he found he didn't mind the coercion.

"Where are we going?"

"To talk to Harvey."

"I just did. He isn't in a chatty mood."

"Well, he's got something to explain, that's for sure."

"Your father was here, checking on Pauline's whereabouts."

She bit her lip. "So we were right that he was worried about her."

Brent wanted to discuss it more, but he didn't figure Donna was about to stop. They arrived back at the porch.

"Hello, Harvey. I went to look at the shed where I saw you earlier. Can you tell me about it?"

He looked at the ground. "No."

She sat down next to him on the porch swing. "I know you feel worried, but you're not in trouble. I just need you to give me the key, okay?"

He shook his head, shoulders slumped.

Donna put her hand gently on his forearm. "You were just trying to help. No one will be mad at you. Please give me the key so I can help, too."

Anxiety pinched Harvey's mouth, and he rocked on the porch swing.

"You're a good friend to Pauline, aren't you?" Donna murmured.

Brent could hardly keep still. What was she getting at? Forcing his hands in his pockets, he clamped his jaw shut.

"Pauline is my friend," Harvey said. "We're going to the Christmas festival at the Del on Christmas Eve. We're going to see the parade and have hot cocoa and watch the ice-skaters, but I don't skate. I just watch, because I don't like to fall down."

"That will be fun. My dad…" She swallowed. "My family goes every year."

The glimmer of sadness made Brent want to wrap Donna in an embrace. He remembered Christmas in the days after Carrie died. The gift she'd never unwrapped. The memories they would never make. The darkness in his heart that would rise up again every holiday season.

"There are fireworks," Harvey said. "Very loud."

"I like that part, too," she said, "but sometimes I put my fingers in my ears."

Harvey blinked and flashed a crooked smile. "Yes, me, too. I made her a present. Do you…do you want to see it?"

"We would love to, Harvey."

Harvey scooted into his apartment, leaving the door open.

"Tell me what is going on here, Donna," Brent said.

She put a finger to her lips as Harvey returned, clutching a handcrafted wooden box painted blue with tiny black paw prints. "It's a box for Radar's treats."

Brent's chest went tight.

Donna beamed him a breathtaking smile. "I can tell you worked really hard on it. Pauline is going to love that."

Harvey nodded. Slowly, he pulled a chain necklace looped through a key from under his shirt and let it dangle from his fingers, not looking at Donna. "Here."

Donna patted Harvey on the back. "That is the right thing to do, Harvey. I'll be back in a second, okay?"

Brent had to jog to keep up with Donna as she raced to the trail between the trees. The physical toll of rescue swimming demanded that he stay in pristine shape. Veterinarians must have similar demands. She wasn't even breathing hard, sprinting effortlessly on legs long and lean.

He was wild to talk to her, but he found himself tossing questions at her back as he scrambled to catch up. "Why are you here? How did you find Harvey? What's in the shed?"

"That's too many questions to ask while I'm running."

"Then take them in order."

"Okay. I was up early thanks to my sisters' predawn visit. I drove here and before I even made it into the office, I spotted Harvey, scooting along, looking over his shoulder as if he was trying to be sneaky, so I just watched him for a while. He was returning from a shed where they store the old landscaping tools and such. I tried to talk to him about it, but he only wanted to go back to his apartment. I met him there and we talked for a while."

"So you went to check out the shed? Why?"

She sighed. "I honestly don't know. Something in his body language was suspicious. Or maybe my sisters are right and I'm desperate to try and be an investigator as a way of handling my grief. I don't know, but my nosiness paid off."

"How?" He managed to keep from shouting the question.

"You'll see in a minute."

They reached the end of the trail. Sitting under a gnarled star pine was a small wooden shed, not often used, judging from the blanket of pine needles on the roof. Across the grass field was a view of the town, still sleepy due to the early hour, and beyond that, the glitter of the ocean. There was one small window, clouded with dirt.

Finally, he caught Donna by the shoulder.

She twisted around, hair swirling in a soft cloud, eyes piercing him with navy blue.

"I'm done being dragged along like a bag of laundry. Tell me," he demanded.

"You're not patient. Isn't that a problem in your line of work?"

"Sometimes aggressive works better than patient."

"That won't help in the veterinarian business. I'm as patient as the day is long." She held up the key for him and he grabbed her hand, imprisoning it in his.

He pulled her a little closer, an electric charge surging through their connected hands. He should let go, but he didn't. "And you're enjoying stringing me along."

She raised her eyebrows in mock innocence. "Would I do something like that?"

"Without a doubt." He eased her fingers open. Her mischievous look suddenly vanished, her tone serious.

"Unlock it and see for yourself."

A thrill of tension shot through him. What would he find? Fragments of old memories coursed through him. Casualties he'd plucked from the ocean a moment too late. A drowned child he'd had to wrestle from his mother's arms, an elderly grandfather whose birthday fishing trip with his sons had turned tragic. A glimpse of Carrie's hair fanned out on the water as the rescue crew loaded him into the boat, him utterly helpless. The muscles of his throat seized up, but he forced himself to look at the facts and allow common sense to overcome the irrational fear. Donna's expression was not one of horror, more of hope. Whatever lay behind the door might show him the path to find Pauline. He eased the key in the lock. It stuck, grating against years of rust and disuse. Slowly, he wriggled the lock back and forth.

Something brushed against the door from the inside.

His pulse raced. The lock grudgingly turned, but the door resisted his effort.

He thought he heard a whimper.

Adrenaline fueled, he rammed his shoulder against the wood.

It gave abruptly and he stumbled across the threshold as something hurtled the other way, knocking him to his knees.

Scrambling to his feet, he saw Donna laughing as Radar barked and jumped, trying to lick her face in a mad frenzy.

Donna finally calmed Radar, after he repeated the same crazed behavior with Brent. Brent knelt, stricken, rubbing Radar's ears. The dog whined, trembling, licking him under the chin. Donna saw Brent's throat convulse and she regretted teasing him earlier.

"How'd you get here, boy?" Brent whispered.

But she knew his real question was about Pauline.

"Harvey told me Radar showed up on the property on November 30 at 3:41 p.m. I'm sure he's right. He's got a thing about dates."

"And Harvey just kept Radar? All this time? He didn't tell the manager or the police?"

"He figured he'd just take care of Radar until Pauline returned. Actually, I think he knows there's a no-pet policy here, but he's been enjoying playing with Radar and caring for him, sneaking him out for night walks and such, he says." Donna ran a hand over Radar's sides. "Radar's been well fed and brushed. Harvey's done a good job."

Brent stood, jamming a hand through his hair. "A good job? And while he's been doing this good job, my sister's been missing?"

"He didn't know he was doing anything wrong."

"All these weeks gone by," he groaned. "Who knows where she could be by now? The police could have been out looking. I would have been searching. She would never leave Radar."

"But this is a breakthrough, isn't it?" Donna said. "My dad was on the right track. Maybe the police can figure out how Radar got here."

"You think?" Ridley said, striding up the trail. "After you interviewed this Harvey resident and took it upon yourself to mess up any evidence we might have gathered here?" His mouth was a hard line.

Radar trotted to meet the officer, then backed away. Donna gave him a comforting pat and hooked her fingers around his collar as a precaution. The poor animal had been through a lot, and that made him unpredictable.

"I'm sorry. My only thought was to free this dog."

"Way to go. Mission accomplished. Now you two need to get out of this investigation and stay out."

"What did you learn from the manager?" Brent said.

"What part of *stay out* did you not understand?"

"It's my sister," Brent shouted, leaping to his feet. His hands were in fists, shoulders rock hard, muscles corded in his forearms. Radar barked. "I'm not asking for your badge and the keys to the squad car. My sister is missing. What part of that do *you* not understand?" The last shouted words echoed through the trees.

Ridley's face softened slightly. He held up a placating palm. "Okay. I get that. I have a sister, too. Manager didn't have much to say. Pauline has no enemies that he's aware of. No disagreements with staff or residents, and as far as anyone knows, she's on vacation, so now you know as much as we do."

Brent's eyes flashed. "She would never go on vacation without Radar."

"Could be she left him with someone and he got loose."

"I don't buy it."

"I don't care," Ridley snapped once more before he caught himself and sucked in a breath. "We will continue to investigate. If something happened to your sister, we'll find out what, but you need to stop muddying the waters. Go home."

"Would you?" Brent said, eyes burning. "If it was your sister?"

Ridley hooked his fingers on his gun belt. "I'm not asking, Mitchell. I'm ordering. I don't want to arrest you."

Brent looked as though he was about to explode.

"What about Radar?" Donna asked quickly. "Can we take him?"

Ridley considered, kneeling to examine the dog, but Radar backed away with a growl.

"He's aggressive?"

"Only when he gets a bad vibe from people," Brent snapped.

"He's been traumatized," Donna put in quickly. "He needs to feel safe before he can be approached by strangers."

Ridley frowned. "All right. Take the dog. I know where to find you when I need you."

Donna removed her belt and looped it through Radar's collar as a makeshift leash. She thrust it into Brent's hands. He needed something to do before he made things any worse. "Let's go."

Brent stared for a moment at the shed, eyes shifting in thought. To her relief, he turned and guided Radar away. They stopped at Harvey's unit.

"You did a great job taking care of Radar," Donna soothed.

"Can't he stay?"

"Not right now, Harvey. We need to take him where he can have his own yard to play in."

"Until Miss Pauline returns, you mean. Radar lives with Miss Pauline, in her yard." Harvey's eyes searched her face.

Donna bit her lip. "Yes, of course. Until Pauline comes back."

"I'm going to miss him. He likes me," Harvey said, patting Radar on the back.

"I'll bring him to visit."

Harvey gave Radar a final pat and watched from the door as they headed back to the parking lot.

Brent was silent and there was really nothing more Donna could think of to say until they reached his motorcycle.

"Maybe Radar should stay at my place," Donna said.

"Dog's coming with me."

"You're living on a boat. He needs a yard to run."

"I'll take him running on the beach."

"He's an eighty-pound animal. He needs room."

"He's coming with me," Brent breathed hard. His gaze dropped to his boots. "I'm sorry. Radar's all I've got."

His only connection to his sister. Maybe the closest he'd ever get to her again. She swallowed the pessimism and touched his shoulder. "How about I give you two a ride to your boat, then, and I'll bring you back to get your motorcycle later?" She squeezed his hard biceps, cajoling. "Unless you've got an extra helmet for Radar?"

He nodded; a sliver of a smile was her reward.

Why did she want to comfort this man she'd hardly met? And why wouldn't he leave her thoughts? She climbed behind the wheel of her SUV. Brent opened the door for Radar, who launched himself into the backseat. The dog let out a bark that made the windows rattle.

"No backseat driving," she said.

As they drove out of the parking lot, both Radar and Brent stared out the window, perhaps with the same question on their minds.

What had happened to Pauline?

SEVEN

Sunlight could not penetrate the clouds as they drove toward the Glorietta Bay Marina. The three docks were filled with a hundred boats of all descriptions, from small runabouts to top-of-the-line yachts, and the public dock was busy with tourists eager to book bay cruises and water taxis despite the weather. Some boats berthed in the harbor were festooned with Christmas lights that would bring the marina to life at sunset. Donna was sucked into the memory before she knew it, the time when her father's marine buddy had motored them out around the bay on a New Year's Eve two years before when the boats were still decked out in their holiday finest.

"Don't have to wait for New Year's," her father had whispered in her ear just before they toasted with cups of steaming cocoa at midnight. "Every morning is a blessing and a clean slate."

She'd been angry at the time, knowing he was praying that she'd detach herself from Nate. It was as if Nate had had some power over her, with his confidence, the way he pursued her, the inconsistent attention that was so intoxicating when it was focused on her. He'd shown up in her world when she was vulnerable and he'd exploited her every weakness. No, she'd let him exploit her. She'd refused the toast her father suggested that night and later met up with Nate, who'd brimmed with apologies for disappearing with his buddies for several days.

"Let's go for a ride," he'd cajoled.

And they had. Too fast in spite of her screams in his ear. He'd lost control thanks to the marijuana she had not realized he'd smoked.

How weak she'd been, how right her father. Thank God that He'd saved her.

"Where'd you go?"

She blinked to find that Brent was looking closely at her. "Just…recalling something."

"Someone, more likely. I'm a good listener, if you want to share."

To share with him? All her humiliation and shame? She shrugged in a "not your business" kind of way. "If you don't mind, I'd like to take Radar for a run at the dog beach. He needs time outside before you coop him up on that boat. I'll bring him back."

Brent frowned. "I'm going to take care of the dog. Don't worry about him. You can just leave us here."

"A quick run on the beach. Then I'll leave." She didn't understand the chill that crept into her body then as she avoided the lustrous brown eyes that sought hers out. Brent was confident in himself, handsome, enticing, just like Nate.

As if to add his support to her idea, Radar snaked out a pink tongue and licked Brent behind the ear.

He laughed. "All right, you big baby. Go for your play-time."

She drove to Ocean Boulevard and squeezed the SUV into a parking place. Radar was quivering with excitement when she led him down to the beach. A sprinkling of rain lent a chill to the air, leaving the shore empty of visitors.

Radar did not seem to mind. When she let him off leash, he bolted to the water, sniffing clumps of kelp and dodging the waves. Seeing him running free and relishing the cool of the morning made her smile.

"Hey," Brent said. "If I was prying back there in the car, I apologize."

"No need."

"There is if I made you uncomfortable." He ran a hand over her arm, which made her shiver. "I don't want to do that, ever."

"Nope. Just fine. I'm going to go give my sisters a call."

"Sure thing."

She practically sprinted up the beach toward the elegant Hotel Del, its rich red roof poking up into the clouded sky. In the distance, a helicopter thrummed. Military exercises from North Island Naval Air Station.

Her bare feet sank into the sand as she put some distance between herself and Brent. Radar pranced happily in the waves and she sneaked a look back. Brent was staring out at the ocean, his own cell phone held to his ear. Hoping for a message from his sister? Had he really felt bad about prying? Or was it that easy charm that oozed out of him unconsciously?

Donna checked her texts as a teen strolled across the grass toward the beach, hands shoved in his jacket pockets.

No change for Sarah. Doctors feel confident. Meeting for dinner at Candace's after hospital. Dragging Mom there at five.

Donna sent a confirmation.

Waves scoured the beach and the rain held at a gentle patter. A little water wouldn't hurt Radar and the poor dog was so thrilled to be outside after being locked in the shed.

The teen had reached the sand, moving toward her, keeping to the firmer sand.

She smiled a greeting.

He did not return the smile. His faded gray eyes were wide; he had scruffy facial hair. His expression, she finally discerned, was both haggard and crazed. And, she realized with a surge of fear, he wasn't a teenager.

Before she could turn and escape, he ran to her and grabbed her by the front of her Windbreaker.

"If you scream," he said. "I'll kill you."

There were no messages, so Brent watched the helicopter circling the water. He'd spent hours in the great shuddering monsters, rotors churning against the worst weather God could dish out. The noisy sixty-four-foot Jayhawks seemed enormous until they were hovering over the massive ocean, looking for a victim amid twenty-foot waves and hurricane-force winds.

"Go get 'em, boys," he muttered, feeling a desire to be aboard that took his breath away. Doing something. Saving someone. Taking control. Another ten days and he'd hopefully be cleared to resume duty, or maybe sooner.

But how could he do that without knowing about Pauline? The uncertainty was killing him, but maybe the knowing would be even worse. No, it wouldn't. He was a rescuer. He would save her.

Radar bounded over and shook himself. Droplets of sandy water shot everywhere and Brent flung up a hand to shield himself.

"You're gonna be trouble, I can tell," he said.

Radar flopped over on his back for a belly rub.

Brent complied. Even the toughest military men, from navy SEALs to army rangers, could not resist a canine belly offered up in trust. His gaze drifted to Donna, and he was surprised to find her talking to someone else. A kid, maybe, or a scrawny adult? Hard to tell through the drizzle and the distance.

Brent stayed put. Donna didn't want him close. That much was certain. No law against admiring her from a distance, though, her hair dancing in the breeze, body slim and elegant against the ocean backdrop. He continued to watch. They must have been well acquainted, as the guy was close. He shifted, Radar whining when the belly scratch was discontinued.

"Hey, boy, want to walk down the beach? Sand looks better over there."

He edged along and to his satisfaction, Radar took off, sprinting ahead, giving Brent the excuse to move toward Donna. The guy was still talking to her and the closer Brent got, the more confused he became.

The stranger was very close, intimate, as if he were sharing a secret with her, leaning in, nearer to that lush mouth. What would Donna see in a scrawny dude like that? His own jealousy surprised him. *Pride talking, Mitchell. They can't all be rescue swimmers, now, can they?*

Trying to pretend as if he wasn't staring, he took another look from the corner of his eye. He'd learned to read body language in his rescue duties. Would the victim panic and dive for their rescuer? Cling with a death grip to the piece of wreckage holding them afloat? Now his nerves were jangling.

Too much tension, stiffness in Donna's shoulders. Not love. Fear.

He sprinted toward Donna and the stranger.

As he got there, the guy let go of Donna and pulled a gun from his pocket.

"You come closer and I'll kill both of you."

The gun shook in the guy's hand. Brent saw now the assailant was in his early thirties, maybe. The red-rimmed eyes, shortness of breath and hollow cheeks spoke of drug abuse. His grimy long sleeves no doubt covered needle tracks.

"You can have whatever's in my wallet," Brent said. "Take it and walk away."

He fixed desperate eyes on Brent. "Your sister had something for me. I need it."

His skin went cold. "How do you know my sister? Who are you?"

"I'm her friend Jeff Kinsey. She was helping me and she left something. I couldn't find it at her place. Did you take it?"

Brent exchanged a look with Donna as the idea hit home. "Were you the one in her basement?"

"No." Jeff chewed his chapped lower lip. "I need it. I gotta get away. She promised."

"Where's my sister?" Brent took a step closer.

Jeff steadied the gun. "Where's my package?"

He heard a roaring in his ears. "If you want something from me, tell me what you did to my sister."

"Don't make me kill you." He tightened his grip on the gun.

"You're gonna have to," he yelled, stepping in front of Donna, "because you're not leaving this beach until you tell me what you did to Pauline."

Radar reacted to the urgent tone and came running toward them at full clip. Jeff swiveled the gun toward Radar. Brent barreled into him, driving his head into Jeff's stomach.

The guy toppled over as expected, but he kept his grip on the gun. Radar's barks rose in a frenzy as he leaped and jumped, uncertain how to proceed. Brent grabbed for the gun hand. Jeff's cold bony fingers clutched it tightly. Donna gripped the back of Jeff's T-shirt and yanked.

"Back off," Brent grunted to her, terrified that Jeff would squeeze off a shot and hit her.

She didn't listen. Now she'd gotten one hand on Jeff's hair and pulled hard. Jeff gasped, wriggling so violently that she lost hold and fell over. The shift in momentum sent Brent somersaulting across the sand. In a moment, all three were on their feet again, Jeff still clutching the gun.

"Gonna shoot you," he said, spittle flinging from his chapped lips.

"You're going to tell me what you did to my sister," Brent commanded, wishing he could tell Donna to run. "Right now."

He saw Jeff's finger hesitate on the trigger. *Better got a vital organ, kid, because I'm coming for you.*

A truck pulled up along the street. Jeff shot it a quick glance and hissed something under his breath. Then he took off running away from them up the beach. The truck idled a moment and then motored away, paralleling Jeff's movement as he sprinted, sending up puffs of sand.

Brent and Donna watched, both breathing hard, until both the truck and Jeff were out of sight.

"What just happened?" Donna whispered. Her hair was hanging in damp waves, her lips parted, eyes wide. If she wasn't so completely attractive, he might have been able to rally a proper head of steam. Instead, he found himself grateful that she wasn't hurt.

"You should have run."

"You needed help."

"No, I didn't."

"He was going to shoot Radar."

Brent glowered at Radar, who had gone off to sniff a scrabbling crab. "Some German shepherd. I've seen hamsters more ferocious than that."

"He's a therapy dog, not a police dog."

Wearily, he took out his phone, dialed the cops and left a message for Ridley. "He'll be thrilled to hear from me again."

"This time, we weren't interfering. Jeff found us."

"Yes, he did," Brent said, his stomach tight. "He's been watching. He was probably the guy who escaped through the bathroom window, which means it probably wasn't my sister we saw that night." Muscles in his throat convulsed. "Was he the one that attacked you at the office?"

"I don't think so. He sounds different."

He took her by the shoulders. "Are you sure?"

Her hands closed over his. "Right now I'm not sure of anything."

And there it was, the twin strands of courage and fear shining in her expression. There was such strength in those eyes, yet at the same time, she was fragile, vulnerable. He pulled her close, burying his face in her hair, arms hard around the softness of her body.

"You could have been hurt," he murmured.

He heard her breath catch. For a split second she relaxed into him, her cheek grazing his, lighting a glow inside him before she pulled away.

"I'm okay."

Two blooms of pink appeared on her cheeks and her lips quivered. He'd done it again. Gone too far. Made her feel uncomfortable. He looked away at the cloud-cloaked horizon to regain his composure and let her find hers.

"What did Pauline leave for him, if he's telling the truth in the first place?" she asked.

It made no sense. "I don't care what she left or didn't leave. I need to know what he's done to my sister."

"Whatever Jeff is looking for could lead us to answers." Donna shoved a tangle of hair out of her face.

"It's more complicated than that."

Her lips were parted, and he forced himself to look instead at her eyes. She had long lashes, and her eyebrows were crimped in thought. "What? What are you thinking?"

"Donna, that truck, the one that took off after Jeff."

She cocked her head, waiting.

"It looks like the same one I saw at your father's office the night you were attacked."

Her mouth fell open in shock. "So I was right? Whatever happened to my father is wrapped up in this, too?"

"Possibly."

She took a shuddering breath. "I wonder if the cops will believe me now."

If only the lead cop didn't have it in for Brent. "Things between me and Ridley are impacting the investigation." He forced the words out. "You'd be better off following your sisters' advice."

"What do you mean?"

"Stay out of it—leave it to the police."

"But you're not going to do that?"

"No, I'm going to follow the trail as long as I can. I'm not going to stop looking for my sister, ever, and that's going to annoy Ridley, which is going to make waves. I'm probably risking my career."

"But rescue swimming is your whole life."

It felt as though he was swallowing a shard of glass. "And it will kill me to lose that, but I have to find my sister."

"We're working together, remember?"

"That was before. You'd better step away. I'm going to do whatever I need to and you don't want to get into trouble working with me on this." He imagined her turning, walking out of his life forever. For some reason, it hurt to think about losing this woman he'd met only the day before. He wasn't ready to hurt again. After Carrie, he might never be. He squared his shoulders. "Anyway, thank you for finding Radar. I'm going to take good care of him, I promise."

An odd smile drifted across her lips, a flush of sudden determination. "Number three is Darius Fields."

"What?"

"The third name on my dad's list in Pauline's file."

"Okay. Thanks."

"And Jeff Kinsey is second."

"And that leaves yours truly as the number one."

"Yes."

"Why are you telling me this now?"

"Because," she said. "We both need answers and the only way we're going to get them is by working together."

"Ridley—"

"Ridley can puff and blow all he wants. My father was a marine. He never gave up and neither will I."

Moisture shimmered in her eyes, her shoulders strong and squared.

A quick electric thrill coursed through his nerves. "So we're going to be detectives," he said slowly, "together?"

"Ooh-rah," she said, whistling for Radar and marching back toward her SUV.

EIGHT

Brent bought some dog supplies on their way back to the Open Vistas after a discussion with Ridley, who met them on Ocean Street before they left the beach. Though Donna was sure Ridley wanted to find fault with Brent, there was no way Jeff's arrival on the beach could be blamed on Brent.

Brent called a buddy to drive his motorcycle back to the boat, but there was no answer. He was ready to dial another number when Donna took the keys and handed him hers. "What are you doing?"

"I'll take your motorcycle and you can take the SUV until you can arrange for something else to cart Radar around."

He stared. "Uh, well, I don't know."

"I've driven everything from motorboats to tractors and plenty of motorcycles. Marco owns three of them."

"Still, I…"

"Are you afraid I'll ding up your bike?" His bewildered expression nearly sent her into gales of laughter. "I promise, I'll be careful. I've been through a motorcycle crash, and I don't intend to repeat the performance."

Donna said goodbye and straddled the bike, pulling on the helmet.

He stopped, Radar pulling at his new leash. "Can I have your number?"

"Is that your best pickup line? Shouldn't you tell me that I'm gorgeous or something first?"

It was his turn to go pink cheeked. "I want to call later and check on you. Jeff may know where you live. He thinks one of us has what Pauline left for him."

She gave him the number and programmed his into her phone. Exchanging phone numbers with Brent? *We're working together. That's what people do.*

Working as detectives? Partners? Was she crazy? No doubt her sisters would confirm that diagnosis. Forcing herself not to watch Brent and Radar return to the slip where their boat was docked, she started the engine. Somehow the admiring look on his face pleased her. It was only a few months ago that she'd tried riding with Marco again, and she held on to her newfound sense of courage. She drove to the hospital and made her way to Sarah's room, where she found her mother and two sisters. They all embraced her.

"They're weaning her off the meds tomorrow," Angela said.

"She'll be home for Christmas," her mother said with her characteristic optimism, stroking Sarah's cheek. "That's good because who else will eat the turkey wings? Only you, sweetie. It's time for you to wake up."

And tell us what happened? Would Sarah realize that their father had died in the accident? The thought of telling her made Donna's stomach plummet. She watched her mother caress Sarah's hand and marveled that she found the strength to both grieve and comfort.

As if she could read Donna's thoughts, her mother looked at her. "Your sisters tell me you've been doing some investigating."

Donna's cheeks heated up. All eyes were on her. She flicked a glance at Angela, wondering if her latest news would best be shared when their mother wasn't present.

JeanBeth Gallagher pressed her lips together in that way that meant resistance was futile. The Gallagher women inherited their determination from both sides. Bruce might have been a Marine Corps Medal of Honor recipient, but no one was more heroic than the woman he'd left at home to raise the family and keep the faith alive, praying for her soldier's safe return. JeanBeth had done everything from nursing her girls through pneumonia to fixing flat tires and washing machines to scaring away a would-be burglar with a baseball bat. JeanBeth was marine-corps tough, even in grief.

Straightening her tailored sweater over her trim figure, she gestured for her daughter to tell the story. "Let's hear it."

Donna plunged into the details, telling everything from the attack at the office to the stranger with the gun on the beach. When she finished, all three women were staring at her in openmouthed astonishment.

"Tell her, Mom," Candace sputtered. "Tell her to quit this crazy business before she gets hurt."

Her mother regarded her through gray eyes that were both tired and resolute. "So you're determined to be an investigator in this matter, Donna? With no training and no one to guide you?"

Donna raised her chin. "Yes, ma'am."

"And why do you think you will succeed in this endeavor?"

"I'm not sure I will, but I know I've got to try."

"Why? Why do you feel that way?" her mother asked.

"Dad taught me to trust my gut and when I didn't do that, I almost lost my life. My gut says to investigate and that's what I've got to do." Her voice shook only a little.

"You see?" Candace said. "It's lunacy. She thinks she has something to prove because of Nate. Tell her to stop, Mom."

Their mother tucked strands of her short bob behind her ears. "It's not her I need to tell," she said calmly, looking at Angela and Candace. "It's you two."

"Tell us what?" Angela said.

"Your father raised you to stick together, no matter what

the conflict. If Donna is going to investigate this, you two need to help her."

Candace gaped. "But, Mom, we're not private eyes."

"There are no other people that care about finding justice for your father more than you girls."

"It's dangerous."

"Don't you think I know that? If Donna is right, then someone is targeting our family. First Bruce and Sarah…" Her voice cracked. She paused, then exhaled. "And now Donna. I know you girls are smart and savvy. Your father taught you to take care of yourselves and you've got good enough sense not to do dumb things. Investigation is research, not running around stirring up trouble. You three can research better than anyone and feed whatever you find to the police to help them."

"But, Mom…" Candace said. "What about this guy with the gun?"

"As I said, research only and none of you put yourselves in any more danger. Marco will be back soon to help and this man…" She looked at Donna. "What's his name?"

"Brent Mitchell," Donna said.

"He's going to be there with you, right?"

Donna swallowed a swirl of feelings. "I think so."

"But he was on Dad's suspect list," Candace said. "He could be mixed up in his sister's disappearance."

Her mother held up a hand. "He's a rescue swimmer. He runs into situations—"

"When everyone else is running out," Candace finished with a huge sigh. "I know it seems that way, but, Donna, Brent could be lying about looking for his sister in the first place to throw suspicion off himself. Do you trust him?"

The question took her breath away. Donna had trusted the completely wrong guy before. It was time for her to make the call and she was grateful that God had given her a family that would allow her to redeem herself. God really was a God of second chances.

"Yes, I do trust him," she said.

Angela nodded gravely. "Okay, then. That's decided. I'll call a few of Dad's old contacts and see if they can help us figure out who this Jeff Kinsey is."

Donna embraced her sister with a rush of excitement. "Thank you for believing in me."

Angela patted her. "I've always wondered what it would be like to be a private eye. Do I need to get a trench coat?"

"You might if this rain continues," Candace said with a laugh. "I'm going to pick up Tracy and I'll meet you back at the house later." She clutched Donna's elbow. "All right, sis. We're with you on this, but I just can't lose anyone else, so be careful, please."

She embraced her sister through her own film of tears. "We're not going to lose," she said. "Not this time."

Brent knew he was stepping over the line. His fingers hesitated on the cell phone again. Next to him in the passenger seat of Donna's car, Radar lay like a lump. Everything drooped, from his tail to his ears, and except for the occasional whine, he was silent.

Brent dialed. Donna answered on the second ring.

"Brent? What happened?"

"Uh, nothing, exactly."

"You're not calling me at ten thirty because nothing happened."

"It's Radar."

"What?"

"Something's wrong with him."

"I'll come. Be at your boat in thirty minutes."

He took a breath. "Actually, I'm in front of your house."

There was a pause. And then a chuckle that lifted his

spirit and seemed to set the world right for a moment. "Well, come in, then."

He led Radar to the porch past a dead poinsettia, limp and desiccated.

In a moment, she'd opened the door, dressed in workout gear of a soft blue. The dog clumped onto the porch with only a halfhearted tail wag, knocking over the poinsettia on his way inside.

Brent righted it. "Sorry."

"Oh, never mind about that. I bought it before…" She waved a hand. "Since my dad died, I haven't been exactly taking care of things at home."

She dropped to her knees and began running her hands over Radar's body, speaking soothingly to him all the while.

She gently palpated his stomach. "Has he eaten anything?"

"No. Not even his kibble."

Radar whined and licked his lips.

"Are you sure?" Her glance was accusatory.

"Yes, and he's been with me every moment," Brent said with a touch of pique.

She listened to Radar's heart. Her hands were so gentle and her words sweet and soothing.

"I should have taken him to the urgent care hospital, but…" But what? He couldn't bear the thought of strangers poking and prodding at Pauline's best friend and he trusted Donna. Completely. For some reason that he could not understand.

"I should run some blood tests."

His gut tightened. "I hear a 'but' in there."

"But I have a theory."

"Care to share?"

"Not right now. I'm going to propose that we watch and

see what happens in the next hour. If he doesn't improve, we'll go to the clinic and do blood work."

"You're the boss," he said, relieved that she appeared relaxed about Radar's condition.

She retrieved a blanket from the closet and tossed it on the floor, and Radar settled down immediately for a nap.

Brent hesitated, looking around Donna's bungalow, which was sleek and modern in cool blues with hardwood floors. "I'll come back, then. In an hour."

She laughed. "What are you going to do in Coronado at this time of night?"

"Go for a run."

"It's starting to rain. Stay here. Can I get you some coffee?"

"Are you sure?" Some part of him was thrilled to be asked by her, but he didn't let it creep into his tone. Cool and easygoing, just like always. "I don't want to be in your way."

"I'm happy for the distraction."

"From what?"

She pointed. In the corner was an artificial Christmas tree, unadorned, the kind with the lights already affixed to the branches. On the coffee table was a wooden cable car ornament, unpainted. "I'm trying to stay in the holiday spirit because my niece, Tracy, will come over at some point and she needs Christmas, but it's…" She clamped her lips closed and blinked rapidly.

"It's hard to feel the holiday spirit when you're grieving." He lifted a hand to reach out to her, but she waved him away.

"Yes, I'm trying to keep it together."

"I understand. Believe me. I lost Carrie two days before Christmas. The lights never seemed to twinkle very bright after that. It's funny how the decorations are the same. All the same singing and activities and things that

Carrie and I used to love to do together, but they just don't touch me anymore." He was floored at himself for sharing those feelings. He'd never let them out of his mouth before.

She poured him coffee, he suspected to keep herself busy. He wasn't sure why he'd blabbered on. The woman was grieving. She didn't need to have him dumping on her.

She put the mug in his hands and brushed against his fingers as she did so. "I'm sorry."

He shrugged, wondering how she'd become the one offering comfort instead of him. "Ridley's right. Carrie was afraid to fly. I coaxed her into it in spite of bad weather. She did it because she loved and trusted me. We were engaged and I was being the macho coastie." Pain stabbed through him but the truth just kept pouring out. "I'd just been accepted to rescue swimmer's school and I was invincible, a hotshot, and I wanted her to see it."

She settled on the bar stool next to him. "What happened?" she asked softly.

"Mechanical failure. Plane broke apart when it hit the water."

"Hard to imagine."

"Yeah. I was conscious for a few minutes. Then I blacked out. At the hospital I asked over and over for Carrie, but I could see it in their faces. Same expression that's on mine when I have to tell a victim their loved one didn't make it." He squeezed the mug in his hands. "That's irony, isn't it? The soon-to-be rescuer lets his fiancée die."

"You didn't let her die."

"No, God did that. What I can't figure out is why He let me live." Why was he telling her all this?

"I wondered that, too, after my accident," she said. "Why didn't I die in that motorcycle crash? Or Nate, for that matter? He was speeding, taking curves too fast. My head just missed the guardrail. Why did God let me live after I flew off the back of that bike?"

He was suddenly riveted on those eyes, the same color as a storm-tossed sea.

"So what's the answer?" he asked.

"To why we're alive?"

"Yes."

She examined his face. "Because God wants us to be. He loves us. He loved Carrie, too, but He had other plans for her."

Brent almost choked on it. "God kills my fiancée and the pilot but not me so I can do what, exactly?"

"Live your life and help others to live theirs."

"If God loved me, He would not have taken Carrie."

"I used to think that kind of thing, too." Her lips tightened in sadness. "It would be easy to feel that God has turned His back on me since Dad died. Years ago, I started into this downward spiral when Candace's husband, Rick, was killed in Iraq. She was pregnant with their second and she lost the baby. Then my mother was diagnosed with breast cancer. I just started to feel this anger that I had done the right thing, been the good girl my whole life, and there was no guarantee for anyone. I met Nate, and he was exciting and fun and he loved being with me. I thought that's the kind of life that I wanted. After the accident, I obsessed about why I was alive. I don't anymore, though."

"Why not?"

"Because there's one fact I can't get around. God let His own son die, Brent, to save us." Her face shone with earnestness that took his breath away. "We're not guaranteed anything, not one single day, not one moment. The only thing I know for sure is that He loves us enough to send His son to die for us."

His own son. Sent to die so others might live.

Live your life and help others to live theirs.

His career was about risking his life so others could live, but he had the sinking feeling he wasn't really living at all. Confusion and pain raged through him, leaving him afire with things he did not want to feel.

She reached out and touched his temple with her fingertips, then traced them along his face. In spite of himself, he closed his eyes, feeling her skin like the smooth silken interior of a seashell. How he wanted that peace that she possessed even through her grief. How he desperately craved that hope that she was right, that he was loved, that Carrie's death and the pilot's were not a punishment.

A fantasy, his mind told him. He moved back, saw the uncertainty in her face and hated himself for making her feel it.

He cleared his throat, put down his coffee and walked to her Christmas tree. "Christmas is a hard time," he said lamely.

"Yes," she said, voice timid, like a little girl. Awkwardness stretched between them and he found himself craving the closeness he'd felt a few moments earlier. He took a step toward her, but she'd already moved to check on the dog.

"The good news is that I think I was right about Radar," she said.

Brent whistled for the dog, who stood and came to him with more energy.

"You all right, buddy?" Brent gave him an ear rub.

Donna put out a bowl and poured some chicken broth into it. Radar eased over and lapped it up.

Relief ballooned inside him. "What was wrong with him?"

She held up a finger. "I'm going to make a quick phone call."

She stepped into the bedroom, leaving him mystified. Donna Gallagher was one maddening woman, which did not explain the ache he felt when he was separated from her.

After a moment, she returned.

"What's the diagnosis?" Brent asked.

"Seasickness."

Brent blinked. "What?"

"He's seasick. From being on your boat."

Brent took a long look at Radar and laughed. "You're a landlubber, Radar?"

Donna's eyes sparked with excitement. "I remembered Pauline mentioning she'd taken him on a whale-watching trip with the Open Vistas residents, and he'd gotten sick as the proverbial dog. By the way, I called my sister to see if she could get us some names of outfits that do whale-watching trips in case it might help us trace Pauline's last steps. It might be a dead end…"

"But it's worth checking out. I'm sure the police will do it as soon as they get around to it."

He was torn between relief, amusement and excitement. Finally, he offered a palm and high-fived her.

"What's that for?"

"Your keen veterinary skills and some great detective work."

She blushed. "Anyway, I think you'd better leave Radar with me. He's not cut out for sailing."

"Seems that way."

Donna checked her texts. "My sister Candace just sent a list of fifteen businesses that offer whale-watching excursions outside San Diego Bay."

"Long list," Brent said.

Donna gave him a sly grin. "No doubt Harvey remembers the name of the company. I'm sure he'd love to visit with Radar tomorrow morning and we can ask him."

"I'm going to have to start calling you Sherlock."

"Fine, Watson. Take your bike, leave my car here and I'll pick you up in the morning so we can take the dog along."

He stroked Radar once more and headed for the door.

On his way, he stopped, drawn to a halt at the foot of her forlorn Christmas tree. Impulsively, he reached out and hung one shiny gold ball on it. "It's more hopeful somehow."

"Yes," she agreed, tears sparkling in her eyes.

Deciding he'd made enough of a fool of himself for one evening, he said good-night.

NINE

"Harbor Tours Deluxe," Harvey said, his face wreathed in a smile as he brushed Radar's coat. "That's where Pauline took us. On November 2. It was a Sunday."

Donna tried to keep her excitement in check as they headed back to the SUV. Brent edged into the driver's seat before she could manage it. She phoned Candace, who was with Angela in the office.

In moments, she had the address.

"It's owned by a D. Fields, it looks like," Angela said. "Wasn't there a Fields on Dad's list?"

"Yes. See what you can find out about him."

"Will do. I got a few things about Jeff Kinsey. He used to be a semiprofessional surfer. Won plenty of competitions. Arrested a few times for drug-related offenses and gradually dropped out of the surfing scene."

Donna shared the info with Brent, who punched up his speed.

"Thanks, sis. I'll let you know what we find out at Harbor Tours Deluxe."

"I don't think it's safe..." Candace started.

"Brent's with me. It's broad daylight. Talk to you soon. Keep me up to date on Sarah." She disconnected before her sisters could rally a protest.

Brent gave her a wry glance. "They're worried I'm going to be a bad influence?"

With my track record, who could blame them? she felt like saying. He seemed to be able to read the dark thoughts racing through her mind. Without taking his eyes off the road, he took her hand and caressed it.

She allowed it, feeling a brush of warmth and comfort.

"You're hard on yourself, aren't you?" he said quietly.

"And you're not?"

"You didn't hurt anyone else."

"And neither did you. The plane crashed. It was not your fault."

He kissed her fingers, lips supple against her skin. "My head knows it, but not my soul, if I even have one."

"You do, Brent. You do."

She wondered if he heard the throb of emotion in her voice. With a final squeeze, he let her hand loose. She regretted the distance immediately.

Think about the case, she chided herself. *Think like a detective, not some smitten teenager. You are not in the market for a relationship.*

They drove across the Coronado Bridge and headed north to Mission Bay.

Harbor Tours Deluxe was run out of a small building in the corner of a wide parking lot. Across the asphalt expanse jam-packed with cars, Mission Bay Marina was gearing up for a holiday boat parade. Though the event would not kick off until the weekend, people lined the docks, decorating their boats in lavish style. The spectators crammed every free inch of space near the harbor, picnicking and enjoying the Christmas music and watching the transformation of the boats.

For a moment, her breath caught as she was bathed in the joy around her, Christmas with all the happy trimmings. Laughter, love, rejoicing. But this year, she would be a grief-stricken observer, watching others celebrate, praying for her sister Sarah's recovery and mourning her father's death. Though she would still rejoice at the gift of her Savior, joy was not the same thing as happiness.

"We picked the wrong day to visit," Brent grumbled, pulling her from her thoughts. He finally found a parking place and squeezed in. Radar was reluctant to get out of the car, so they left him nestled on a blanket in the back, windows half-open to provide some ventilation.

They snaked their way through the cars across the lot. Donna was grateful for the relative quiet.

Brent pointed to the sign on the door. "Closed."

"Too much going on to keep the business open?"

"I guess." He cupped a hand and peered into the darkened window. "I can see lights in the back."

She followed him as they edged the building around to the back. The door was open a few inches, the interior dark. Brent raised an eyebrow and subtly crept in front of her, slipping into protector mode.

Paint peeled off in a clump under his knuckles as he knocked.

From inside, something thudded against the walls hard enough to make them vibrate.

"Door slamming?" she whispered, her cheek against his hard shoulder.

He knocked again, louder. "Hello? Anyone in there?"

There was a smash and a groan. Brent was across the threshold before she realized he was moving. Readying her phone to dial the police, she raced in after him down a short dark hallway. The sound of breaking glass reverberated in the dark space.

They pounded into what must be the front office. A big man with a shaved head, bat raised in his hand, jerked in their direction. Another man, dark haired with a trickle of blood running down his face, stood across from them, a hand raised to protect his head.

Brent picked up a wooden chair and shoved it at the man with the bat. "Stop," he roared.

Then the bat arced through the air at Brent as the guy switched gears. It smashed into the chair and broke the spindly legs. He swung again and Brent ducked. The bat whistled over his head and cracked into the Formica counter.

"Get out, Donna," Brent yelled. In his haste, he slipped on a puddle of water coming from a shattered fish tank and went over backward. The next blow would crush his skull.

She ripped open her purse, and grabbed her pepper spray. As she brought her hand up to aim the spray, the man batted it out of her grip with a closed fist. The impact stung her wrist and sent both the container and her purse flying. Brent was on his feet, eyes burning as he punched. The blow glanced off the man's chin and drove him back stumbling.

Brent pressed his advantage, shooting out a foot to catch his attacker's ankles. The move should have toppled the goon, but he caught himself on the counter before he went down.

He dived under Brent's outstretched arms and barreled out the door. Brent whirled and raced out, Donna after him.

They emerged into the parking lot to find no sign of him through the milling people and slow-moving vehicles. Brent jogged warily through the aisles of parked cars. Donna did the same, peering underneath in case he was hiding there. With a shudder, she recalled the feel of the cold hand that had grabbed at her feet from under the office table. Swallowing her fear, she pressed on.

Now Brent was leaving the parking area, working his way toward the last dock. At first she couldn't see any sense to his actions. It was clearly under repair, roped off with a "closed for refitting" sign. Missing boards showed along the narrow dock. The section was old, run-down, the last of the docks waiting to be upgraded. There was no escape for the intruder in that direction.

Though she hurried to catch up, Brent was still far ahead of her, beginning a wary examination of the deserted dock. His shoulders hunched, as if he was listening.

She patted her pockets to find her phone, then remembered she had dropped her purse back at the office.

"Brent," she called. "I need your phone."

He was too far away to hear. She started to move closer when Brent froze, then crept to the edge of the weathered planks. Transfixed, she saw him suddenly vanish as something pulled him off the dock and into the water.

Brent hit the water feetfirst, the impact driving his breath from his body. The bay was not a challenge for Brent, not compared to ocean and without the rotor wash from a helicopter, but his assailant was another story.

He immediately dived, his intention to swim underneath and take the guy from behind, as he'd been trained to do with panic-stricken victims. This man was a seasoned fighter and not suffering from panic. He kicked out hard, impacting Brent's forehead, making his ears ring. Fighting his way to the surface, Brent realized the guy had hauled himself into a dinged-up motorboat. Brent shot through the water and grabbed for the stern, but the man managed to cast off and motor away.

Brent fumed, treading water, watching him leave. "Yeah, you run. If you come around again, it's gonna be a different story." He realized that he was filled with rage not for his own struggle or the boat shop owner's but over the fact that the assailant had struck out at Donna.

Donna was probably only bruised, but he could not rid himself of the anger that someone had threatened her. Again. He tried to restore a sense of calm with the steady churning of his arms and legs. "What is the matter with you, Mitchell?"

His existence since Carrie's death had been about rescuing victims. Rescue deployments usually resulted in a quick black-or-white outcome. He got them out alive, or he didn't. Though some victims stayed with him, stuck in his gut, Donna was another story entirely. He could not seem to pry her from his thoughts, and the ferocious need to protect her baffled him.

"Brent," Donna yelled, her stricken face appearing over the side of the dock. "Are you hurt?"

"Only my pride," he called up. He swam easily to the nearest ladder and hauled himself out of the water onto the dock, where he stood gushing all over the planking. "What about you?"

"Me? I'm not hurt."

"Let me see your wrist," he demanded.

Chagrined, she held out her arm.

He ran wet fingertips over the smooth surface, feeling the pulse ticking there.

"This is a little ridiculous, considering you're the one who got yanked into the bay." She peered closely. "Your forehead is bruised."

Brent wiped water from his face. "He got off a lucky kick. Won't happen again. Gonna go see if the guy in the shop is okay."

He was grateful that the visitors to the marina were so engrossed in the festivities that they did not pay much attention to a dripping-wet man slogging through the parking lot.

They reentered the shop the way they had the first time. "Everybody okay?" Brent called as they returned to the front office. The man he assumed was Darius Fields sat on a chair now. A small woman with long dark hair held an ice pack on his face. She let out a scream and grabbed the can of pepper spray. "Get away," she rasped.

"Easy, we're the good guys," he said.

Her features were pinched in fear. She had a long nose, dark eyes, small mouth; she was probably in her midthirties. "Who are you?"

Brent made the introductions and explained what had happened. The pepper spray in her hand wavered. He liked to think it was his friendly charm, but it was more likely Donna's encouraging smile.

"Thank you for helping Darius," she finally said, lowering the spray. "I'm Fran Mercer, his fiancée. Did you come to book a whale-watching trip?" she said.

"No." Brent bobbed his chin at Darius. "We wanted to ask him a few questions and found some guy beating up on him. We should call the police. My phone's waterlogged."

Donna reached for her bag.

"No," Darius said. "It was just some thug, looking to rob us. Happens all the time and I don't need the bad publicity now, at Christmastime."

Brent frowned. "I'm not comfortable with that. He came after us, too."

Darius shrugged. "Look, I can't stop you if you want to bring in the cops, but as a small business owner, I'm asking you for a favor. The economy's rough. I need all the visitors I can get. What did you come here for, anyway?"

"I'm Pauline Mitchell's brother. Do you know her?" He watched their expressions carefully. Maybe he imagined it, but he thought Fran's lips tightened a hair.

"Pauline?" Darius considered while gently probing the lump on his temple. "Oh, yeah. She booked a whale-watching trip here for a group home, I think."

"In November," Fran said. "I do the books, so I remember the name." She fingered her hair. "Why are you asking about her?"

"She's disappeared."

Again the slight ripple of unease crossed Fran's face. He wondered if Donna saw it, too.

"Man," Darius said. "That's too bad. I haven't seen her since that day. She was a nice gal. Had a dog, I remember. The tour group seemed to like her. Sorry I can't help you find her, but I got my own problems."

"Please," Donna said, and Brent wished she didn't have

to look so beautiful when she approached Darius. "We think her disappearance is related to my father's murder."

"What?" Fran gasped.

"His name was Bruce Gallagher. He was a private detective. Someone caused his car to crash and it killed him and nearly killed my sister, who was driving." Donna took a gulping swallow. "She's in the hospital in a coma."

Fran pressed her fingers to her mouth and looked away. "That's horrible."

"Hey, I'm sorry about that. Don't know your dad," Darius said.

"We're going to find out what happened," Brent said, "and we're going to find my sister. We would appreciate anything you could tell us."

He threw down the ice pack. "Wish I could, but I only met her the day she came to book the trip. I stick to boats and try and stay out of people's personal lives." There was something bold in his tone, almost as if he was daring them to contradict him.

Fran picked up the ice pack. "You should sit and keep this on until the swelling goes down."

Darius laughed and cocked an eyebrow at Brent. "See what happens when you get yourself a fiancée? They start to think they own you."

"She's right," Brent said. "You should keep the ice on."

He shrugged. "I'd love to take the day off and coddle myself, but I have to go pick up a part and rig up our boat with some lights. It's Christmastime, you know."

"Aren't you afraid the guy will come back?" Donna said.

"I'll be ready next time," Darius said.

"But what about Fran?" Donna blurted.

He laughed. "She's tougher than I am, aren't you, Frannie?"

She looked down. Darius gave her a hug and pressed a

kiss to her temple. "I'm joking, baby. Everything is going to be fine. I'll be back in an hour. Call me if you're scared about anything."

The door slammed shut behind him.

Brent looked at the small woman. "Do you know something about my sister?"

"No, nothing." Fran wiped at a bead of moisture on the counter. "Listen, I've got so much to do today it's mind-boggling, so I really need to get started."

"Are you sure you want to stay here alone?" Donna said.

Fran darted a look at her and then out the window to the departing Darius.

"I'm fine," she said. "I'm used to it."

Brent grabbed a piece of paper and a pencil and wrote down his number. "When my phone's back up and running, you can reach me on my cell." He hesitated. "Fran, it's not my business, but are you worried about Darius?"

She blinked and stepped back, shoving the paper in her pocket. "That is none of your business but for the record, Darius is right. I am tougher than he is."

She turned her back on them. Brent and Donna left the shop.

"Do you think he's lying?" Donna said.

"Yes, maybe her, too."

"Is she afraid of him?" Donna stared at the boats and the milling crowd.

He touched her shoulder. "What's on your mind?"

"I feel like I'm missing something."

"Me, too."

A truck passed, Darius at the wheel. He turned his head, giving Donna a long look and a smile that made her shiver.

"He creeps me out."

He continued on, waving to some people on the dock.

A lightbulb flashed in Brent's head. "His truck. I recognize it now. He was the one following Jeff Kinsey after he went after you on the beach. Could be that it was Darius's truck at the office the night you were attacked, too."

Her face paled. "Why would Darius attack me in the first place? I've never even met him."

"I have no idea, but I'm going to find out."

TEN

Brent agreed to drop Donna at the hospital. On the way, her muscles tensed with each passing mile. She couldn't get Darius's smile out of her mind. She again felt the memory of that knife pressed to her throat.

Little girls who think they're tough like men. You know what happens to them? She swallowed, fighting her way back to the present.

"I'm going to tell Ridley to check out Darius's truck. I'm going to tell him about the guy at Darius's office, too, no matter what he says," Brent was saying.

She nodded. "Good idea."

He pulled up at the hospital. The tension tightened her stomach into a tight fist.

"Are you gonna be okay?"

"Yes." She blinked hard against the pressure of tears. "No. I don't know."

His hand found hers. "Tell me."

She fought for breath. "They're going to wake Sarah up today and it's likely that she doesn't know how…how things turned out in the crash." Her throat convulsed.

"You're going to have to tell her that her father is dead." His tone was gentle.

"Yes. And even worse than that, she was the driver." She closed her eyes and sagged against the headrest. "I can't stand the thought of telling her."

Brent sighed. "That's rough."

"It's like reliving the whole thing over again." Tears fell now, coursing down her cheeks.

He handed her a tissue.

She clutched it. "Just when I finally stopped crying every moment of the day."

"I'll come with you, if that will help."

His brown eyes were soft with compassion and it almost loosed another flood of tears. She realized with everything in her that she did want him to come, to hold her hand, to stand steadily beside her against the storm front she knew was coming. She craved his company…as she had with Nate?

He reached up and gently wiped the tears from her cheek. "I hate to see you grieving."

Her senses surged into a rising tide of longing. She wanted him to be there in that hospital room, but it was not the time to seek comfort from a man. Not now, when she had her head back on straight, and not now, when her battered family was about to fall apart once more. She caressed his hand against her cheek for a moment and then inched away, reaching for the door handle.

"I really appreciate that offer, but it's better if I go alone."

He nodded. "I understand."

"Feel free to put Radar in my backyard. He won't like driving around all day and there's a lot of room for him to run. I watched my neighbor's dog last week, so there's a bowl next to the garage. Be sure he has some water. Let's wait awhile on offering food to be sure his nausea is gone."

Brent smiled. Again her pulse ticked up a beat. "Always thinking like a veterinarian."

"It's what I do." She shook her head. "It's the only thing I have to offer."

His face went serious. "You're wrong there, Donna," he said. With one finger, he traced the trail of a tear from the corner of her eye around the swell of her cheek to her chin. His touch left a path of warmth that bubbled through her.

Face hot, she got out and closed the door. The strange

mixture of feelings followed her up to the third floor, where her mother and sisters were already gathered. She saw at once she was too late. Sarah's eyes were wide, red rimmed, her face blotchy. Angela held one of her hands and their mother held the other. Candace stood at the foot of the bed, her own face twisted with grief.

"Oh, no," Donna murmured.

Sarah's eyes riveted on hers, dazed "They told me," she gulped. "I know he's dead. After… When I was trying to unbuckle my belt… I could tel… I killed him. I killed him."

Donna drew close, touching Sarah's knee. "No, honey," she whispered. "Don't say that."

Sarah did not appear to hear, nor did she react to the reassurance from the women gathered around her. "He wanted to go visit a beach up north to check something out. I laughed and said yes, but only if I could drive." She stared at the wall somewhere above Donna's head. "Dad is…was…such an aggressive driver."

It was true. Their father drove with all the intensity of a heat-seeking missile.

Donna waited, breath bottled up inside.

"I…was driving up Highway 1. There was a car," Her eyes clouded with grief and pain. "It sped up and rammed into us from behind. I couldn't keep the car on the road."

"Don't think of it," Candace cried. "It's over. It was an accident. Don't torture yourself."

"She needs to remember," Angela said quietly.

Candace bit her lip.

Their mother gripped Sarah's hand. "You listen to me, Sarah Cassidy Gallagher. You grieve, you rage if you must, you cry your heart out, but you are never to blame yourself for your father's death. It just happened and we have to live with it, to live through it." She bent her head and started to pray, but tears choked off her words.

Angela finished the prayer.

Donna offered her own grief in a prayer, imagining it circling upward. There was comfort in knowing her father was already with God, but comfort did not mean the anguish was any easier to bear. She added one more request. "Lord, help me find out the truth." The truth might be the only way her family would ever heal completely.

Sarah fastened burning eyes on Donna. "I heard Mom on the phone." She swallowed and JeanBeth held a cup of water for her to sip. After a moment she resumed. "You are going to find out who hit us and why. Is that right?"

Donna nodded. "I'm trying."

"Do better than try," Sarah said, voice low. "You have to find out."

Doubts assailed Donna fast and furious. *I don't know what I'm doing. I'm floundering. I'm not a detective.*

"Find out. Please." Sarah closed her eyes and began to sob again.

"I will," Donna said with more confidence than she felt.

Candace and Angela were looking at her now.

"We will," Candace said.

And that was when Donna felt the brush of the Lord's comfort. She hugged and kissed her mother and sisters and stroked Sarah's hair, and they cried for a good long while together. When Sarah fell into an exhausted sleep, Donna, Angela and Candace stepped out into the hallway. Her sisters looked as wrung out as she felt. She filled them in on the day's events.

"We have to find out what Dad was looking into," Angela said.

Candace fingered a strand of her curly hair. "When Sarah is calmer, the police will want a description of the car that hit them. That might help."

A thought wormed its way through Donna's haze. "Why the beach?"

Her sisters stared at her.

"Why would Dad suddenly want to go to some beach? He wasn't a 'hang out on the beach' kind of guy. What was his interest in doing that?"

Angela raised an eyebrow. "I'm not sure, but here's something that might help." She held up a phone. "It's Dad's. The police returned it to us today. I know he kept notes on his phone sometimes."

Donna's heart thudded. Her father had been the tech king. Every new phone or gadget sent him into little-kid excitement. She remembered standing in line with him for hours to secure the newest version of his smartphone. The smile had never left his face. Her throat was suddenly clogged with unshed tears.

Candace gripped her arm. "We'll check out the phone. You and Brent see what you can find out on your end about Pauline."

Donna nodded, not trusting her voice.

"Invite Brent to my house tomorrow night," Candace said. "I'm going to try my best to give Tracy some Christmas cheer. She's been begging to decorate a gingerbread house. We could use a dinner guest."

The thought of bringing Brent along, almost as if he was a date, gave her a tickle inside. "I can see the wheels turning in your head, Candace. He's looking for his sister. There's nothing between us, nothing personal."

"Of course," she said in an innocent tone that irritated Donna to no end.

"What should we do about Sarah?" Donna finally managed.

"We'll take shifts and stay as long as they'll let us," Candace said. "I'll do the first one. You go take a look at the phone, Angela. Dad's..." She cleared her throat. "Dad's charger is at the office."

Angela sighed. "You know, I never imagined I would be a private investigator."

"Neither did I," Candace said. "But then again, I never imagined I'd lose my dad five years after I lost my husband." Her expression was so bleak that Donna engulfed her in a hug, her heart breaking all over again.

Angela wrapped her arms around them both and Donna realized how thin her sister had gotten. Together, the sisters clung to one another, holding tight, their grief mingling along with their strength.

"We're going to get through this," Donna said fiercely. "I promise."

With God's help, the Gallagher sisters would find some answers.

Brent clutched the bushy poinsettia plant as he regarded Donna's front door. What was he doing? She'd think him too forward or a fool. He was undoubtedly both. He couldn't even explain to himself why he'd bought the thing.

Just leave it and go.

There was no need to tell her who it was from.

A secret-Santa gift, his sister used to call them. How had he managed to become Santa?

He put the plant down and picked up the dead one. Then he put that one down so he could adjust the new plant into a slightly more pleasing spot on the doorstep. Did poinsettias like sunlight or shade? Would Donna come home to find the scorched remains?

"The more sunlight the better for poinsettias." Brent jerked to find an elderly man walking a well-groomed corgi.

"Is that right?" he said stupidly.

"Yes. They're natives to Mexico, so the sun will do nicely."

"I see. Thank you, sir."

The man saluted and continued on his way.

Feeling even more the fool, he retrieved the dead plant

and edged the new one with his foot farther into the sun. It toppled over. Muttering, he was stooping to fix the problem when he heard Donna's laughter.

He straightened so fast he managed to drop the dead plant.

"Are you trying to teach my poinsettia a lesson?" she said, twirling her house keys in her hand. "I think that specimen has already given up."

His stomach fluttered. Caught, when he'd been so close to making a clean getaway. "I…uh…"

She peeked around him and got a glimpse of the lush blooming plant on the porch.

Her mouth opened in surprise. "You didn't bring that for me, did you?"

Great. She really did think he was too forward now. Why hadn't he just left the thing and run? "Yes, I did."

"Why?"

Her blue eyes glimmered. He swallowed. "I know things are hard for you and your family. My mother always said it wasn't Christmas until you had a poinsettia on your porch." He heaved out a breath. "I wanted you to have some Christmas."

She clenched her arms around her middle and he knew he'd blown it. She would tell him nicely to butt out of her personal life. He'd overstepped. Then he noticed she was trembling and two patches of high color had appeared on her cheeks. Tears streamed unchecked and she began to sob.

Way to go, Brent. The instinct to rescue reared up again and he took the keys from her hand, unlocked the door and ushered her inside.

"What can I do?" he murmured. "I'm sorry."

She didn't answer, her hands clutched to her mouth. He could not think of anything else to say, so he pulled her to his chest and held her close.

"Oh, Donna. I didn't mean to make things worse," he murmured into her hair.

Her breath came in shuddery gasps and she melted into him, her forehead pressed to his chest, tears wetting his T-shirt. The embrace assaulted him with memories of all he had lost, of a woman who used to trust him to comfort her. He had not realized what a precious honor that was until he'd lost Carrie. Now, somehow, he'd been given the chance to comfort another amazing woman. It was dizzying. And terrifying. He wanted to both run and hold her close at the same time.

Comforting, not anything more, he told himself. It was just part of working as a team. In rescue swimming you were only as good as your pilot and flight mechanic. He was strengthening the team, that was all.

When her sobs subsided, he led her to the sofa. The house was cool, so he draped a blanket around her shoulders. While she huddled there, he made his way to the kitchen and heated water for tea. There were no proven benefits to having tea in a crisis, but he'd noticed women seemed to find comfort in the ritual. He searched the cupboards until he found some and dunked a bag in water for what he hoped was an appropriate amount of time before he brought it to her.

She took it. "I'm sorry. I'm not much of a crier, usually."

"No problem. I'm, uh, very sorry. I thought the plant thing was a good idea at the time."

"It was," she said, lips trembling. "It was so incredibly sweet, Brent. I can't tell you how much it means to me. And you're right. Christmas is coming and my father was the biggest fan of Christmas of anyone I know. He would be horrified if we overlooked the blessings because of the grief."

His chest tightened. "I wish I had met you years ago."

She shook her head. "I was busy messing up my life."

"Isn't that called growing up?"

A smile appeared on her face, like the sun overcoming the clouds.

And then he was moving toward her, his mouth seeking her lips, heedless of anything but the desire to burn away the lingering sadness. His lips brushed hers for a split second, the shock of electricity pulsing through him, until she jumped away.

His senses jangled for clarity that his brain could not provide. He had no idea why he'd tried to kiss her and why his body cried out at his failure. He only knew he could not undo what he'd just done.

"I...apologize."

"Oh. It's okay." But there was now a wall between them. He could see it in her eyes. Probably a good thing, since he was clearly behaving like a lunatic.

"How's Radar?" he said, getting up and walking to the window.

"Take a look." She cleared her throat.

They watched him scampering around the backyard chasing a squirrel.

"I'm pretty sure the squirrels are laughing at him," Brent said.

She smiled again, but the tension still shone on her face. He felt like kicking himself.

His phone buzzed. He answered. A wave of icy cold shuddered through him.

"What is it?" Donna asked.

It was as though her voice came from far away. He could not answer at first. She squeezed his arm.

"Brent, please tell me."

He somehow found himself answering. "They found Pauline's car." He swallowed, mouth suddenly gone dry. "The trunk is locked. They're going to open it now."

ELEVEN

They arrived at the empty parking lot within moments. The police were assembled in the far corner of the lot behind a sporting-goods store that was closed for renovations. Piles of wood and buckets of nails littered the lot. No wonder no one had noticed an out-of-place vehicle there. Pauline's car stood doors gaping open while police photographed it from every angle. Ridley watched as an officer went at the trunk with a crowbar.

"Don't have to be here, Mitchell," he said, with a softer tone than Donna had ever heard him use before. "I would let you know whatever we find out here."

Brent didn't answer, staring with burning eyes at the trunk.

"Old car. Doesn't have a trunk release, so we'll have to force it. Store owner reported the car when he came back to check on the renovation progress. Company's been shut down for a few weeks since they're doing improvements."

Donna touched Brent's forearm and found him tense as steel. She had no idea what to say. Here they were, watching a possible nightmare unfold right before their eyes.

What if they found her? Nausea licked at her. All this time, they'd been rushing here and there, following leads that got them nowhere, while Pauline might have been dead the whole time?

No. She clamped her chattering teeth tight and prayed to God that the car would not contain the sad remains of Brent's sister. She kept on praying as the crowbar grated against the metal with a noise that made her skin crawl.

Ridley tried again. "This might not...go well." He eyed

Brent. "No shame in stepping back. Might not be a good memory to keep."

"I'm staying here," Brent said quietly. "Right here."

Ridley nodded at his officer to continue.

The cop shoved the prybar in again and hauled down on it.

With a pop, the lock gave way. The sound echoed like a gunshot.

Brent stiffened but did not move.

Ridley strode up and peered inside. He turned to Brent. "Take a look."

With what must have taken every ounce of courage he possessed, Brent moved forward. Donna stayed back. It was a moment for privacy that stretched unbelievably long. Brent's shoulders slumped. With agonizing slowness, he turned around.

"Empty," he rasped.

She felt her own knees shake as she moved to him. He bent over and sucked in some deep breaths.

"Thank You, God," she heard him murmur.

Thank You, God, she echoed fervently. He straightened and wrapped her in an embrace, his breath warm on her neck. Her mouth tingled as she thought of their earlier kiss. She hugged him tight until he set her back.

"I've got to find my sister," he muttered. "Now."

Donna's phone buzzed and she answered. "I'll check it out," she said before she disconnected.

"News?"

"It's Silver Cove—that's the name of the beach where Dad and Sarah were heading. Angela found the name on Dad's phone. It's up the coast a ways. It's small, and you have to access it by trekking over some rock formations, from what my sister can tell online. I can't imagine why he'd be going there."

"So we should look."

She hesitated. "I can take Radar. We'll be okay by ourselves."

He shook his head. "Don't shut me out."

"I'm not sure—"

"I know I shouldn't have kissed you earlier and I apologize. What's happened recently, and here just now..." He sighed. "It's turned me upside down. I apologize that I made you feel uncomfortable."

"You've got good reason to be off balance, but I just want to find out the truth and support my family. That's all." No relationships. Period.

"Understood, and I need to find my sister, now more than ever."

"Okay. We'll go together."

Donna continued to mentally reprimand herself as they went to the car. Brent should not have tried to kiss her back at her house, but she definitely should not have desired him to. Prickles erupted along her spine at the memory of how close he'd been, how much she'd wanted to share a kiss with him. Solving a case and tending to her family: those had to remain her priorities. She did not trust herself to allow an incredibly handsome man into the picture for anything other than investigation purposes.

"I'll drive," Donna said.

He shifted. "It's not a problem—I'm fine."

"I know, but I want to drive." It restored her sense of balance to slide behind the wheel.

Brent huffed. He kept his eyes on the road as they headed north toward the tiny beach. A thoroughly recovered Radar stuck his muzzle out the open window, breathing in the sea-scented air.

She wondered if she should try to discuss what had just happened, the horrible moments waiting to look into that darkened trunk. What he must have been feeling, she could only imagine. Brent stared steadfastly out the window, resolutely silent, so she followed his lead and stayed quiet.

They had to consult the directions as they neared the exit that led down to the beach. "A half mile more," Brent said.

They exited the freeway and took a series of turns that brought them farther away from the residential area. Fewer and fewer cars sped along the one-lane road, which became even narrower. Donna parked and they headed on foot along a rocky trail. It took some effort to climb over the low cliff that led down to the small crescent of beach hemmed in by the rocky wall. Radar scampered ahead.

"It's almost like he's been here before," Donna mused.

"Yeah. I was thinking that, too."

The sand was hard packed under their feet, and the wind made the air brisk. Donna zipped her jacket. "So why here?" she mused. "Why would Dad have wanted to come here?"

"Pauline must have mentioned to him that she liked to come here. Look." Brent pointed to a small motorboat rounding the spit of rock that formed the cove. He squinted. "I saw that boat tied up at Darius's place."

He took her arm and they stepped back into the shelter of the rock wall.

The boat came closer and Donna gasped to discover that it was indeed Darius Fields piloting the craft. He let the engine idle, bobbing on the whitecaps.

"What is he doing?" She peered closer, taking a pair of binoculars from her pack. "Brent, he's got something in his hands."

"What?"

She blinked in disbelief and looked again. "Roses. He's scattering roses in the water."

They stared at each other. Darius stood in the boat, swaying.

"He's drifting. The boat's going to knock against the rocks if he doesn't take some action."

The vessel floated awkwardly in the grip of the waves. Brent started out of concealment. "He's not in control."

A figure approached down the cliff trail, a small woman whom Donna finally identified as Fran. She stopped when she saw Brent and Donna, a cry escaping her lips a moment later as she caught sight of the boat. "I knew it." She looked at them. "I... Nobody's ever at this beach. Why are you two here?"

Brent ignored the question. "What's the matter with him?"

"He's been drinking," she said. "I was working on the books. He came in and grabbed a jacket, and I could smell the beer on his breath." She blinked hard. "I tried to catch him before he took the boat, but I wasn't fast enough." She chewed her lip. "I saw someone else, another boat I didn't recognize, take off after him."

"Was it the guy who roughed him up in the shop earlier?"

Fran shrugged.

"How did you know he would come here?" Brent asked.

Fran flushed. "It's a familiar place to him. His mother drowned near here and he comes all the time and drops flowers into the water."

Donna didn't know if she believed the story or not. Darius did not seem to her to be the sentimental type. Then again, people, like dogs, could be something altogether different than they appeared, which probably explained why during her years as a vet she'd been bitten by only tiny little cute-as-a-button furballs. The big, brutish dogs were often teddy-bear sweet.

Brent appeared to be only half listening, his attention riveted on the wandering boat. "Can you call him?"

Fran dialed her phone. "No signal. I'll climb up on the rocks."

Brent moved toward the surf. "Might not matter. In a minute, he's going in. There's an undertow here. How strong a swimmer is he?"

But Fran had already climbed up the rock wall. When she came to a flat place that jutted out over the ocean, she stopped to take out her phone.

Brent was now close enough that the water lapped his feet. He took off his jacket and shoes.

"You're not going to swim out there," Donna said.

"Only if I have to. We'll wait and see if Fran can get him on the phone. Maybe we can talk him back in if he's sober enough."

The waves crashed against the sand. Donna was a strong swimmer, having grown up in the ocean since her father and mother introduced her to the surf when she was a tot. Still, she did not like to think about fighting through the waves to get to a drunken man who did not seem like the cooperative type.

Come on, Darius. Answer your phone.

An orange vessel rounded the point, flying through the salt spray. "Is that the coast guard?"

"No. It's a RIB," Brent said. "A rigid inflatable boat," he added to answer her next question. "And it's heading right for Darius."

"To help?"

He didn't respond. "Binoculars?"

She handed them over.

Brent peered for a moment. "It's the guy who was going after Darius at the whale-watching place."

Donna could hardly process what was happening. As if in slow motion, the orange inflatable rammed into the motorboat. Darius tumbled headfirst into the water.

Brent crashed into the surf. Donna was amazed at his

speed. In a few steps he was waist deep in water, swimming powerfully through the whitecaps. Radar swam after him, barking, until Donna called him back.

"Darius," Fran shouted from above. Her voice was twisted in fear.

There was a sound of rock giving way and Fran plummeted feetfirst into the ocean. In horror, Donna saw her resurface for a moment, dazed, until the waves began to tug her away from shore.

Donna did not bother to shout for Brent. He would not hear her, nor could he leave his first victim to help a second.

She plucked off her shoes and shed her jacket. It was Donna's turn to race into the surf.

Brent stopped to get his bearings. With no flight mechanic to help coordinate the rescue from above, he was on his own. Ahead and to the left, Darius floundered, his arms slapping ineffectually at the water.

Brent made straight for him. "I'm going to help you. Calm down and tread water. I'll tow you to shore."

Darius's eyes were blurry and unfocused. "Get away."

In his peripheral vision, he saw the orange raft approaching again. The pilot grinned. There was no more time for dithering.

Brent grabbed Darius and attempted to put him back in the motorboat, but Darius grabbed an oar that had fallen overboard and swung it at Brent. He ducked and delivered an open-palmed smack to Darius's forehead. Enough to stun him. Momentarily, he loosened his hold and Brent ripped the oar from his fist.

The raft was upon them now.

"Boss told you to pay up, Darius," the pilot said. "Do it, or you're dead," he shouted over the waves.

Darius yelled something unintelligible. The pilot pointed

the craft at them and bulldozed forward, a wicked smile on his lips.

Fury nearly choked Brent. He swung the oar as the boat drew near, cracking it against the pilot's kneecap. The pilot screamed and went down. In a second he was up, throwing himself against the starboard side and grabbing for Brent. Brent evaded the grasping fists. He wanted to lash out again with the oar, take the guy down a second time, but Darius was going under, the cold and alcohol working against him.

Brent struck away from the RIB and lifted Darius's face out of the water. He came up in a panic, clawing at Brent.

"Stop it." Brent manhandled him into a rear head hold and making for the beach. The RIB cut them off, circling to get between him and the shore. Tenacious. Whatever Darius had done, he'd angered the wrong people.

The boat idled there as the man considered his next move. They were running out of time. Brent could swim easily for the shore, but Darius could not.

"Are you coming back for more?" Brent shouted. "Fine by me. Coast guard will be here in two minutes and you can take it up with them," he bluffed.

He saw the guy flinch and he knew he'd won. Whoever this was, he didn't want to stick around. He scanned the shoreline and a crafty look came over his face.

"Maybe when the coasties arrive, they can save your girlfriend for you, Boy Wonder."

Girlfriend?

Brent whirled back to face the shore. Donna was not there. Away and to his left he caught sight of her swimming toward the point, her head just visible over the waves. Fran must have fallen and Donna must have gone after her.

His instinct was to strike out immediately and help her, protect her, sacrifice himself if necessary to save her.

But he had a victim to rescue.

Everything in him strained to go to Donna. It seemed as if his soul were churning through those waves with her, his heart inextricably bound to hers.

Don't lose her. Save her.

Instead, he grabbed Darius and swam with all the strength and speed he could summon toward the shore.

TWELVE

Fran was unresponsive when Donna finally made it to her. She checked for a pulse and felt a tiny thrumming in her carotid, or was it the trembling in Donna's fingers? She flipped Fran onto her back and began to tow her in, but the current seemed to have other plans.

For every foot of progress, the water swept them back toward the open sea. Radar paddled out to her.

"Good boy," she gasped.

The dog chomped down on Fran's jacket and began to tug. Was it a game to him? Or did he somehow know the humans needed help? She didn't care.

Radar's added strength made all the difference. Donna kicked as hard as she could, stroking with one arm while the dog kept up his share of the load. They were within fifty feet of the shore, still in deep water, when Brent made it to them.

"Can you swim back on your own?" he said.

She nodded.

Radar let go and Brent held on to Fran. He ordered Donna and Radar to go ahead of them. So he could make sure they made it back, she realized. Indeed, it took all her remaining reserves of strength to haul herself up on the sand and she fought against pain in her back.

On the beach, Brent laid Fran down next to Darius, who was sitting up.

He crawled to her on hands and knees. "Frannie."

Brent pushed him away. "Get off and let me check her out."

Donna was relieved when he sat back. "She's breathing on her own."

Radar trotted over. He sniffed at Fran's hair and made his way to Darius, who swatted at him. Radar stiffened, the scruff of hair on his neck rising, and he barked furiously at Darius.

Brent pulled Radar off, but he continued to bark, darting closer to Darius and then away when Brent ordered him back.

Donna finally grabbed Radar by the collar and hauled the dog away down to the surf, where he began to chase some seagulls that had arrived. When she was reasonably sure the dog was distracted, she returned to Brent, who was finishing up his 911 call.

Fran had started to mumble and shiver. Brent climbed back to the car and returned with a blanket, which he draped over Fran, and his jacket, which he wrapped around Darius, continuing to monitor both victims.

Darius patted Fran's hand. "Wake up, Frannie. Why'd you have to follow me, huh? I told you a million times to leave me be."

"She was worried about you," Donna said. "Drunk people shouldn't be sailing. Why did you come here?"

He didn't look at her. "Told you a million times," he repeated softly to Fran.

"Who do you owe money to?" Brent asked.

Darius still did not look at them, just crooned softly, swiping a hand under his nose.

"He needs to sober up," Brent said in disgust.

Paramedics made their way down the trail and took over. Brent and Donna were given blankets and were crowded away from the victims.

Donna watched Darius's abandoned boat making its haphazard journey out into the Pacific Ocean. "Radar seems to know this beach, and Darius does, too." Pieces of the puzzle swirled around in her mind. "Pauline brought Radar here. It's pretty coincidental that this place happens to be significant to Darius. I don't think I buy the 'roses for his mother' bit."

Brent was quiet, lips drawn tight.

"What's wrong?"

"You shouldn't have gone in after Fran," he snapped. "It wasn't smart. You're not trained for water rescue."

"And you're not trained as a vet, but you're helping tend to Radar."

"Don't be facetious. This isn't funny." He rubbed at the water dripping from his hair.

"I'm a strong swimmer. Everything turned out fine."

"You made things more difficult. Added victims to the water."

"You couldn't have saved both Fran and Darius."

"Yes, I could. I do it all the time. It's my job."

A flame of anger ignited in her belly. "Why are you lambasting me?"

"You made a bad choice."

She folded her arms across her chest. "So you're the only one who can be a hero?"

"I'm not…" He broke off, nostrils flared. "I'm not a hero. I do what I'm trained to do. You put yourself at risk."

"So you always yell at Good Samaritans who try to help?"

He hitched his hands on his hips. "I am not yelling. I'm just upset."

Upset, she wondered, or something else? The corners of his mouth pinched; shadows under his eyes showed evidence of sleepless nights. The anger in her belly cooled. She cocked her head and considered, watching the muscles work in his strong jaw and the flicker of something deep in his eyes. "I think, Brent Mitchell, that you're scared."

He gaped. "Scared?"

"Yes."

"This is what I do all the time in conditions way worse than this. Why would I be scared?"

"Because for a minute you felt helpless to save Fran and me." She reached out to touch him. "And helpless is the worst thing you could possibly feel because of what happened before."

He blinked, his mouth twitching.

"I don't need you to rescue me," she added softly. "I'm not Carrie."

A long moment stretched between them and she knew she'd crossed the line. What made her feel the need to probe Brent's psyche?

Then his self-control returned, he huffed out a breath, and he stepped back from her, turning toward the sound of the police siren.

"Think what you want, Donna," he said. "This isn't about what happened to Carrie."

Oh, yes, it is, she thought. Her heart broke a little bit for Brent Mitchell, the man who couldn't save his fiancée.

She shivered. Would he endure the same terrible situation with Pauline, too? She said a prayer that he would not have to face such a horrible truth.

Brent marched to Ridley, eager to put Donna's accusation behind him. She was way off base ignoring responsibility for her own hazardous choice. His anger was justified, not born of some shadowy phantom of the past.

"Ridley," he called.

Ridley glowered at him. "And here you are again."

"Saving lives, if it means anything. Darius would have drowned or been mowed down." He retold the events of the past hour. Donna joined them as Ridley approached Darius.

"You need to come with me, Mr. Fields," he said. "We're gonna have a nice chat after you sleep it off."

Darius shook his head. "Didn't do anything wrong. Gonna stay with Frannie."

"Your girlfriend is going to the hospital. We'll have the medics check you out and then you're going to jail after we give you a Breathalyzer."

His head snapped up, and he glared at the officer. "No way. I'm not going to jail."

"I'm afraid you are," Ridley said calmly. "Operating a boat while under the influence is a misdemeanor in California, in case you didn't know."

"I'm not going to jail ever again," he snarled. "Not gonna get locked up like an animal."

"I beg to differ."

Darius lashed out toward Ridley, but the officer stepped easily aside and Darius fell facedown. Ridley was on him in a moment, handcuffing him. Darius sat up, sand caking his face.

"Don't make it harder than it has to be, buddy," Ridley said. "You're looking at a $1,000 fine right now. Resisting arrest is a whole other level of fun."

Darius got to his feet, looking down at Fran. The trail was too steep to allow the paramedics to take her by gurney, so they had called for a helicopter. Medics loaded Fran onto the aircraft and it roared away.

"You get well, little girl," Darius called. "I'll be there soon."

Brent heard Donna gasp. Her face was pale, her mouth round with shock.

He took her arm. "What?"

It took her a few tries to get the words out. "You," she said, staring at Darius. "You called me little girl that night, didn't you?"

Darius shrugged. "Dunno what you're talking about."

"You were the one who attacked me in my dad's office. You shaved your beard. I knew there was something familiar about you."

His eyes narrowed slightly. Then he offered a slow smile. "You must have me mistaken for someone else."

"No, I don't. It was your truck on the street at our office, and you attacked me."

"Yeah?" he said with a leer. "And how are you going to prove that, Detective Donna?"

Brent put an arm around Donna's waist and pulled her away from Darius. Something in the man's look was tainted and Brent wanted her distanced from it. She clutched his arm with chilled fingers.

Ridley handed Darius over to another officer. "We'll find out," he said to Donna. "While we've got him in custody, we'll figure this all out."

She nodded.

Ridley surveyed the beach, watching Radar nosing around the sand. "Something happened here. Too bad the rocks can't talk."

"Or the dog," Brent said.

"Yeah." Ridley pulled his gaze back to Brent. "Got something for you. Jeff Kinsey, the kid who messed with you on the beach, worked as a dishwasher at Open Vistas."

Brent's nerves snapped to attention. "Yeah?"

"Manager says he's a mechanical genius, too. Fixed everything for the residents in his off time, but he's a drug addict, so they had to can him when he missed too many days of work. He came in pretty beat up one day before he got fired. Your sister was a good friend to him. Took him to the doctor. Loaned him money and such. Helped him find another job after Open Vistas, but I don't know where yet."

Brent forced out a breath. "That's my sister. Her husband was hooked on pain meds, so she knows how the addiction story plays out. She'd want to help."

"So we've got an APB out on him. It's a small island. We'll find him."

"If he's still here," Brent groaned. "He thinks my sister left a package for him somewhere, but if he's given up on finding it, he might have left town."

Ridley looked offended. "You know we Coronado cops do talk with other law enforcement professionals in the outside world. I said we'll find him, and we will." Ridley stalked back to the beach.

Brent called to Radar and started to guide Donna toward the trail, his gut twisted tight with worry. There was no doubt in his mind that Pauline had taken Radar to this beach. And now Donna was convinced that Darius Fields was her attacker. Worry began to claw deeper. Sarah Gallagher's life almost ended. Pauline missing. Donna in danger.

What had Donna told him her attacker had said?

Those little girls die.

He swallowed the fear he'd felt at seeing her fighting against the ocean, so small in the gaping maw of the sea. Girls had died on his watch before, one who was meant to be his future. *Not again.* He wasn't giving his heart to any woman ever again, but he sure as shooting wasn't going to lose another one on his watch. Pulling her closer to his side, Brent led Donna up the rock trail, desperate to find his sister and determined more than ever to protect Donna Gallagher.

The next morning, brilliant sunlight streamed through the blinds and awakened Donna. She lay in bed for a while, trying to breathe away the tension that sprang to life in her body. Radar was pacing in the family room, the click of his nails on the hardwood relentless, so she forced her body into motion. Her phone showed no messages, and she felt a surge of disappointment. Forcing Brent to confront his feelings had been a mistake, a huge overstepping on her part. The man was already worried beyond belief about his missing sister.

Was Darius responsible for Pauline's disappearance? His cruel smile danced in her mind. He was the masked intruder; she knew it with dead certainty. Part of her had known it all along. He wanted her to stop investigating, but was he afraid she'd find out the truth about Pauline? Her father? Or maybe both? Head spinning, Donna made up her mind to go to the police station and talk to Officer Ridley without Brent. She wasn't sure Brent wanted to work with her at the moment. She fixed herself toast, which she had no appetite for, and fed Radar. She put him in the backyard with plenty of water and a new chew toy.

Her phone buzzed with a voice mail message from Candace. "You're bringing the gingerbread house tonight, right? Tracy is asking for it. And you're bringing Brent, too?" Her tone became morose. "We've got to keep our minds off Sarah and the hospital, just for one night. I'm worried about Angela, too. She's all skin and bones. Please come. You've got to."

She wanted to call her sister and say Brent wouldn't be coming. Why would he want to with everything that had happened? Leaving the bad news for later, she messaged back that she would be there with the gingerbread house and all the candy for decorating.

She grabbed her keys and drove to the corner grocery store, where she piled a basket full with frostings and a premade gingerbread house. It stirred up her pot of guilt when she considered she'd always made the pieces from scratch, rolling them out with Tracy's help. Even in the years when she'd felt estranged from her family, who despised Nate, she'd built that gingerbread house with Tracy. Well, okay. It wasn't going to be homemade, but it would be decorated to the nines. She added extra bags of colored candy pieces and a foil Santa complete with nine reindeer pals.

As she headed toward the register, familiar faces nodded and smiled pityingly at her. Hank, the store owner, a retired sailor and longtime friend of the Gallagher family's, approached and embraced her, basket and all. She struggled for composure in his well-padded hug, with the scrape of his whiskers as he pressed a kiss on her cheek. He pulled her to arm's length. "How are you holding up, kiddo?"

"As best we can," she managed, eyes burning.

"Bruce was the finest soldier I ever served with. One of the best men I ever met."

"Thank you."

"If there's anything I can do," he said, eyeing her basket. "That's for Tracy, isn't it?"

She nodded, unable to trust her voice.

He took the basket from her hands and bagged the contents. "On the house."

"I couldn't, Mr. Henricks."

"I insist. Bruce never took a dime when he tracked down the clerk who helped himself from my till. Please," he said, his voice growing soft. "I know what it's like at the holidays when you lose someone. Tracy needs some joy. I would be honored if you would allow me to do this." He drew himself up straight and tall, the proud marine.

She kissed his bearded cheek. "Thank you so much."

He nodded and escorted her from the store, then opened her car door and deposited the Christmas bundle on the passenger's seat.

"You drive carefully, now, Donna. Gonna be praying for the Gallagher family this Christmas."

The kindness overwhelmed her. There was still joy and goodness and plenty of reason to get down on her knees and thank God for her blessings. Even now, even with a heart twisted by grief.

She was signaling to pull away from the curb when

Brent appeared around the corner, dressed in sweats and a T-shirt. He did a double take when he saw her, hesitating a moment before he sauntered over to the car.

Nerves tingling, she rolled down the passenger window. He draped his elbows over the door. "Hey."

"Hey."

His eyes scanned the bagful of gingerbread supplies. "Doing some baking?"

"Yes. Tonight I'm going to put together a house with Tracy after dinner. I'm not really in the mood, but I'm going to summon up some holiday cheer if it kills me." She swallowed hard. "Would you like to come? My sister Candace would love to have company to even things out." She knew her cheeks were flaming.

"Uh, well, I'm not sure."

"I apologize for what I said on the beach. I was out of line."

He stayed quiet, his chin resting on his arms. "I'm mixed up, about everything." There was such desperation in his face she yearned to embrace him.

His sigh was heavy. "I just need to find my sister and figure out what happened to your dad."

And nothing else. No personal attachments. "I understand."

"I was going to the police station after I finished my run to find out what Ridley pried out of Darius."

"Me, too, after the gingerbread supply mission."

He looked again at the contents of the bag. "I guess, I mean, it would be nice to share a family meal. I've been living on takeout and breakfast cereal for the past week."

"I can't guarantee it will be gourmet, but I know we can top takeout and cereal." She held her breath.

"Yeah, okay. I appreciate the invitation. I'll be there."

"Great. Candace will be thrilled."

And, Donna realized, so would she. Just to have him

there as a work partner, if that was all that they were meant to be. Just to be near him. She moved the bag to the backseat. "Hop in. We'll go harass Ridley together."

He grinned. "Excellent. Do you want me to drive?"

"You have a problem not being behind the wheel, don't you?"

"Only a small problem."

"Get in and buckle up. It's time you got over that hang-up."

THIRTEEN

She drove to the Coronado Police Department on Orange Avenue. Officer Ridley gestured wearily to two chairs across from his cluttered desk. "I figured it wouldn't be long before you both showed up. Nice of you to come together." His eyes narrowed and Donna thought there was a sly implication in the tone. Behind him on the desk was a framed picture of a woman with tousled hair, grinning from the deck of a boat. She saw Brent flinch when he noticed it.

Carrie.

Her face was alight with fun, a light speckling of freckles dancing across her nose. Both men had loved her, but she'd chosen to marry Brent. Bad blood simmered between the two men below their straight-faced exteriors.

"Any prints on my sister's car?"

"So far just Pauline's and Jeff Kinsey's, but we're still working on that."

"What did you find out from Darius?"

Ridley tapped a pen on the desk. "Not much from him, but I've been digging. He's got a clean record except for a two-month jail stint three years ago for assault. It seems Darius likes to gamble and he's racked up some serious debt. Darius says he borrowed money from a bad dude to pay off his debt. He refused to name the guy but we're thinking it's a longtime thug by the name of Albert Indigo. Indigo wants his money back, so I surmise he sent his goon over to collect. Guy's name is Mooch."

"It suits him."

"Darius said he had the money ready to deliver to Mooch, but it was stolen by none other than Jeff Kinsey."

"What?"

"Yeah. Pauline talked to Darius and got Jeff a job with his boat company when he got fired at Open Vistas."

"So Darius did know my sister better than he let on," Brent said.

"He says they met a few times to go over trip details before she took her charges on his boat. She even went on one of his cruises to check it out before she booked, so he saw her a few times, anyway. Won't cop to any more than that."

"What about Fran's story that his mother died on that beach?" Donna asked.

"That one was easy. Darius won't speak about his mother, but records show his mom and dad divorced when he was ten. She remarried and is living in Tijuana. Dad kept custody of the three boys. He was a dealer at a casino until he died ten years ago."

"I wonder why Fran lied about it," Donna murmured.

"Could be that's what Darius told her. We did some checking on her, too. Family in Texas, one sister, married with three kids. Dad owns a tiling business. Fran's a part-time paralegal. Makes a decent living. Got her own place in Imperial Beach, but she stays with Darius in this apartment above his shop." Ridley shook his head. "Girl has some smarts and she stays with a guy like him." Again Ridley's eyes flicked to Brent and then away. "I'm guessing Darius will come up with the thousand-dollar fine and be out by tomorrow."

"That's insane," Brent nearly shouted. "You know he's the guy."

"What I know and what I can prove are two different things," Ridley said, his tone flat and hard.

The skin on Donna's neck prickled as she considered Darius would be a free man in a matter of hours.

"What about the attack at Pacific Investigations?" Brent demanded. "He's the guy. Donna is sure of it."

Ridley shrugged. "No prints in the office. It was dark. Guy was wearing a ski mask. You and Marco didn't think to get a plate number from the truck out front."

"So a positive ID doesn't make a difference?" Brent snapped.

"If we had one, which we don't, except for the fact that he's got an alibi."

"What alibi?"

"Fran. She said they were spending a quiet evening at home." Ridley heaved out a sigh. "Now, isn't that convenient?"

Brent stewed on the way to the hospital. There was no question that they needed to speak to Fran. Was she a liar or another victim? Darius was the one responsible for his sister's disappearance; he grew more certain with every passing minute. He was relieved that Donna was too distracted to insist on driving, so he pushed the speed limit and got them to Sharp Coronado Hospital quickly.

"I think you should let me talk to Fran," Donna said.

"Why?"

"Because you are so intense right now you're scary, and you'll make her clam up."

He realized she was right. He was practically sprinting along the hallway after they checked in, and his expression was furrowed into a scowl. He forced himself to relax, slow his pace. "I keep thinking about those roses in the water. Pink roses. My sister's favorite. I've sent her pink roses every year on her birthday since she turned eighteen."

Donna's eyes widened. "It could be a coincidence."

He heard in her tone that she didn't believe it any more than he did. He was practically jogging by the time they reached Fran's room. Donna grabbed his wrist. "Please don't go barreling in there like a Stormtrooper. Women don't like to be accosted by angry men."

"Right." He took a breath and gestured for her to go in first. "After you."

She knocked on the door and stepped in.

Fran was sitting up, sipping from a cup of water. Her eyes went round with surprise. "What are you doing here?"

"We came to see if you're okay." Donna offered a smile. "The nurse said it would be all right to visit for a few minutes. My sister is here, too, recovering from her accident."

"I hope she's getting better." There was a long scratch on Fran's left cheek.

"She's made improvements. The doctors are optimistic, but even if they weren't, we are."

Fran nodded. "I have a sister. She's in Texas. I miss her like crazy." She sniffed and Donna handed her a tissue. "She always stood by me no matter what idiot thing I did."

"How are you feeling, Fran?"

"I have a slight concussion, so they're keeping me for a few more hours, but I'm totally fine. Um, thank you," she said. "For jumping in after me. I guess you saved my life." She giggled. "Maybe you should join up with that guy and be a rescue swimmer."

Brent went for a smile. "She could do it. No question."

Donna patted her arm. "I didn't pull you out by myself. Brent and Radar helped."

She plucked at the blanket tucked around her knees. "Anyway, it's all okay. I'm glad no one was hurt."

Brent could keep still no longer. "It's not all okay. Why did you say Darius was with you the night Donna was attacked?"

Her mouth fell open. "Because he was. I told the police the truth."

"No, you didn't," Brent said.

She started. "Darius was with me. We were watching old videos. He never went anywhere."

Donna edged in front of Brent. "What are you afraid will happen if you tell the truth?"

She bit her lip. Her hand trembled and water splashed on her blanket. "Nothing. I'm not lying."

"Are you afraid he'll hurt you?" Brent said.

She clamped her mouth shut.

"The police can protect you," he said.

"From Darius?" She let out a dry laugh. "I've been in love with him since I was sixteen. I don't need protecting."

"You can love someone who isn't good for you," Donna said.

Brent heard the throb of pain and shame in her words. Very gently, he pressed a hand between her shoulder blades. *Old mistakes*, he wanted to say. *Don't let any jerk from the past make you doubt yourself.*

"Darius is going to be my husband, see?" Fran said. She thrust her ring finger up so they could see the slender gold band. "I'm never going to say anything bad about him."

"It's not too late," Brent said. "You haven't married him yet. He's a liar and he knows something about my sister's disappearance and probably Bruce Gallagher's death, too."

"Get out," she said.

"Do you know what I think?" Brent pressed. "I think he hurt my sister, maybe killed her. He throws pink roses into the water because they were my sister's favorite and he was in love with her."

"Stop it." Fran's eyes flashed.

He knew he should stop, but he could not. "You know what happened, don't you? Did he hurt her?"

"Brent," Donna warned.

"Where's my sister, Fran? Where's Pauline?"

"I don't know anything about this," she cried.

"Whatever Darius did to her," Brent said, "he's going to do to you, too, someday. You've got to tell me the truth before it's too late."

"Get out," she shrieked, face mottled, eyes burning.

A doctor came through the doorway. "You'll have to leave now," he said in no uncertain terms.

Furious at himself and Fran, Brent stalked out the door and down the corridor.

Donna caught up with him.

"I know what you're going to say," he snapped. "I blew it. I should have listened to you."

"Well, yes, you should have, but I understand how you feel." He looked into her clear blue eyes. It wasn't just about him. He'd blown her chance to find out more about what Fran knew about her father, too. He hung his head. "I'm sorry. I'm so angry that it's making me lose control."

And then her arms were around him. He found himself embracing her, burying his face in her waves of silken hair, taking comfort from her warm breath against his neck, the sweet caress of her fingers on his shoulders.

"It's okay."

It wasn't okay. The situation was as wrong as it could be, yet in the bleach-scented shadows of that hospital corridor, something felt completely right, the way it had long ago when he'd been head-over-heels in love with Carrie.

Even as he embraced her, the thought sent a trail of panic through him. *Protect her, rescue her, don't love her,* his brain screamed, even while his heart sought hers. He found his lips grazing along her neck, trailing her jawline. She had only to tilt her head an inch and he would capture her mouth with his.

Back off, his mind insisted.

Donna, how do you do this to me? Why do I let you?

Her body fit perfectly into his embrace, as if they were two parts of one whole. He was dizzied, out of control. He felt a shiver run through her.

Carrie's last scream reared up in his memory. With shaking hands, he pulled her to arm's length.

Her lips were parted, cheeks flushed, and his chest tightened.

"I…" She gave a little shake. "I should go check in on Sarah while I'm here. Would you like a ride back to your boat after?"

He forced his mouth to answer. "Yes. Thank you. I'll wait in the lobby."

She hesitated. "Um, actually, why don't you come with me?"

He searched her face.

"I think…it feels like the deeper we get into this, the more our families are somehow connected. I wondered if maybe you would like to meet Sarah."

Did he? No, he told himself. He was already dangerously close to Donna, strangely tied to her in ways he had not sought and did not want to acknowledge. Seeing her sister vulnerable, the family stricken with worry, was a far cry from building gingerbread houses and engaging in holiday banter. Banter, he was ready for; bonding, not so much. "I'm not sure that would be a good idea."

Her expression wavered. "Oh, of course. No problem. I'll meet you at the car, then."

She headed for the elevator.

His feet were cemented to the floor. He wanted to keep his distance, to step back from the edge where the messy tangle of emotions lay—the deeper levels of a relationship, where he had managed not to go since Carrie's death. Yet his instincts tugged him toward her.

As the elevator doors dinged open and Donna entered, Brent sprinted and caught up, snaking through just before the doors slid closed. She looked at him, but he kept his gaze fixed on the floor buttons. "Changed my mind," he mumbled.

"Why?" she said.

He thought about Pauline, out there somewhere, scared,

maybe dead if he was honest with himself. Carrie gone too soon. Why *was* he there, standing in the elevator with Donna Gallagher, when there were so many reasons to detach himself from her and the peace she stubbornly clung to?

A thought flashed in his brain. Was it possible that he was there, standing in that rising elevator, because he was meant to be?

To rescue her? To help? *Why am I here?*

Her earlier words came back to him. *Because God wants us to be. He loves us. He loved Carrie, too, but He had other plans for her.*

Pain for Carrie twined together with longing for Donna. He cleared his throat. "To be honest, I'm not sure," he said. "I just feel like I'm supposed to be here. With you. Right now." He maintained laser-beam focus on the buttons as they announced their arrival on the third floor.

He felt her looking at him.

"I'm glad," she said simply.

And he found he was, too.

FOURTEEN

Sarah was asleep when they arrived. Angela greeted Brent warmly and JeanBeth clasped his hand between hers. "I know you must be so concerned about your sister's whereabouts," she said. "Please know that whatever we can do to help you find her, we will."

Brent's lips twitched. "I appreciate that, ma'am."

"Has there been any progress?"

Sarah stirred on the bed and opened her eyes.

"Hey, Baby Gal," her mother said, using their father's longtime nickname for her.

Donna blinked tears away. "How are you feeling, sis?"

"I think some dynamite went off in my head," Sarah groaned.

"Been there a time or two," Brent said.

Donna introduced Brent to Sarah.

"I'm sorry about your sister," Sarah said.

"Thank you. I'm certain I'll find her."

Donna knew he had to be wondering if his sister would be found alive.

Sarah's eyes narrowed and she struggled to sit up higher on the pillow. "You believe my father was killed because he was asking questions about Pauline's disappearance?"

Brent shot Donna a questioning look.

"Tell me," Sarah said. "My father died not two feet from me in that car." Her voice faded to a ragged whisper. "I have a right to know."

Donna swallowed against the ache in her throat and nodded to Brent.

He cleared his throat. "Yes, I do believe your father was killed by whoever messed with my sister. We confirmed your father was at Pauline's workplace, Open Vistas, asking about her."

"That's what you think, too, Donna?" Sarah asked.

Donna nodded.

Sarah's face darkened. "I had a lot of time to think last night, since I am a prisoner here. I remembered something important, so I called Angela. The car that hit us was a green pickup."

"Green?" Brent blurted.

Donna understood his outburst. Darius drove a black truck and Fran's vehicle was a white Corolla, as far as they knew. "Are you sure, Sarah? Positive?"

Sarah nodded, wincing as the gesture caused her pain. "Yes, my memory has kicked in as the brain swelling has gone down. It had personalized plates, SURFER1. I noticed because he was following kind of close and Dad commented."

"Did you see the driver's face?" Brent asked.

She shook her head. "Not really. I didn't pay that close attention. Dad might have, but…" She gulped, blinking against the memories from the crash.

"I gave the information to Ridley last night," Angela said. "He's going to be here any minute to tell us what he found out."

"Why didn't you text me last night?" Donna demanded of Angela.

"I wanted to check it out first to see if the information would get us anywhere before I spread it around," Angela said.

"You should have called me right away."

Angela's lip curled. "I'm new at this investigator thing, Donna," she snapped. "Have a little patience, why don't you?"

"I'm trying, but you aren't helping by keeping me in the dark."

Angela stiffened. "That wasn't my intention."

"Time is critical. I could have worked on that lead last night."

"As I said," Angela continued, her voice tight, "I called the police and this investigation is not all about you, by the way. We're all involved here."

"I know it."

"We've all lost a father and everyone in this room wants the case closed for Dad and for Pauline."

Donna was about to fire off a retort until she noticed the fatigue lines around Angela's mouth, the shadows under her eyes. She normally wore her brown hair pulled back in a chic knot, but today it was loose and untidy, as if she'd attempted a quick shower in between shifts at the hospital and office. Trying to be the emotional and spiritual support for three high-strung women in the midst of their worst crisis ever was not an easy task. Angela knew about gritting it out through pain.

She forced a breath in and out and squeezed Angela's hand. "Thank you for contacting Ridley."

Angela squeezed back, her posture relaxing, and something inside Donna relaxed, too.

"Marco called," JeanBeth said. "He'll be back tomorrow. He's been worried about everything going down here. I gave him an edited version, but I think he knows I've deleted some things. He seems to think," she said with a smile to Brent, "that you might be nosing about in the family business," she said. "Those weren't his exact words, but I edited for decency."

Brent chuckled. "He doesn't trust me."

"He doesn't trust anyone," she said. "Especially if he imagines they're a threat. He's a little protective."

"Just a little?" Brent joked.

Ridley stuck his head in the doorway and rapped a knuckle on the jamb. "Is it okay to come in?"

"Of course," JeanBeth said. "Please tell us you've got something positive to report."

Ridley shifted under JeanBeth's direct gaze. "Yes, Mrs. Gallagher. We ran the plates."

They stared at him. Donna held her breath.

"The car isn't registered to Darius Fields or Fran Mercer."

Donna's heart plunged. Had she been wrong? The accident was just that, an accident? "I was so sure it was Darius," she murmured.

"It's registered to someone else you know," Ridley said.

"Who?"

"Jeff Kinsey."

Brent blinked. "Not Darius?"

"Kinsey?" Angela said. "The guy who threatened you on the beach?"

"Yeah," Brent said. "His prints are all over Pauline's car, too. And he might have been the one we saw running from my sister's house with a suitcase full of her things."

"Why would he do that?" Sarah said. "Could it mean Pauline's alive?"

"Imprisoned," he said quickly. "I'm sure she's alive and he's got her stashed somewhere."

Donna heard the spark of hope in his voice and she prayed that his words were true.

Brent finished his thought. "My sister might have hired Bruce because she was scared of Jeff. He didn't want your father to go looking for her, so he forced your car off the road."

"It doesn't explain Darius's bizarre behavior or the fact that I'm sure he was the one who threatened me at Dad's office."

"No," Brent admitted. "It doesn't."

"This case is like some sort of science-fiction monster,"

Angela said, her face grave. "You cut off one head and it grows another one."

"We know Kinsey was trying to get something from Pauline, and his vehicle caused the accident. That's enough, isn't it?" Donna said.

Angela frowned. "I'm new at this investigation stuff, but I'm thinking that just because it was Jeff's car doesn't prove he was driving it."

"We've already started tracking his movements," Ridley said. "He came to the area last year. He's been staying at different campgrounds along the coast until he hits his limit and then he moves somewhere else. We'll find him and bring him in."

"You said that yesterday," Brent fired off.

Ridley glowered. "I've got these rules I've got to follow, Mitchell. It takes longer when you do things by the book."

"My sister's time is running out."

"You don't get to direct this operation. You're not in control here."

"Maybe if I was, Kinsey would be in custody and telling everything he knows."

Ridley smirked. "You're not going to be the hero and swoop in for the big save and that just sticks in your craw, doesn't it?"

Donna saw a nerve jump in Brent's tight jaw.

"I don't care who saves her," he said. "I just want my sister rescued, and I want to know the guy looking for her isn't letting his personal feelings get in the way."

Ridley's nostrils flared. "Watch it, Mitchell. You're close to an accusation that you don't want to make."

"Find my sister."

"I will, but not because it helps you in any way." The tension between Ridley and Brent was palpable, a crackling electric animosity.

"Just help her," Brent said, tone harsh.

"I will." Ridley nodded to the women, turned on his heel and left.

An awkward silence descended in the hospital room.

Brent stood like a coiled spring, hands on hips, staring at the floor.

"I'll tell Marco everything we've learned as soon as he arrives," Angela said. "He's been doing this investigation thing a lot longer than we have. He'll probably think of an avenue we haven't explored yet."

Brent finally looked up. "I'd appreciate that."

More awkward silence. Donna broke it by kissing her mom and sisters. "See you at Candace's."

Brent raised a hand and offered a tight smile. "It was good to meet you all."

"Will you come for dinner tonight?" JeanBeth asked.

Donna held her breath.

"I don't want to intrude."

"You won't be. We'll need all the hands we can get because Candace is a notoriously bad cook."

Brent smiled. "I guess I could come by, if you're sure."

"We'll expect you at six," JeanBeth said.

Outside in the hallway, Donna caught his arm. "Really, if you don't want to go, I completely understand. I'll make excuses for you."

"Somehow I don't think Mrs. Gallagher is the type to accept an excuse very readily."

Donna laughed. "You're right. But still, don't come if you don't want to. I know your heart is somewhere else."

He sighed. "I guess there's nothing more I can do tonight to help my sister. The least I can do is show up and help yours try and muster up some Christmas cheer."

Donna felt a warm glow inside that partially dispelled the pervading sadness. A little cheer. It would not change anything or alter their horrific circumstances, but just having Brent with her would be another reminder that there was still reason to be grateful, a tiny glimmer of Christmas in a very dark season.

Impulsively, she reached up and kissed him on the cheek.

Best of all, he let her.

FIFTEEN

Brent whiled away the hours making notes on his iPad of everything he knew about the case. It was a mess of facts and lies, he was sure. Pretty much everything Darius and his girlfriend said was not to be trusted. He searched the names of all three suspects on the internet without much result. Finally, he slumped over the deck rail, staring out at Glorietta Bay. Across the water, some small boats were taking advantage of the break in the rain, and he imagined he could hear the distant strains of holiday music from the nearby high-rises. Christmas, in all its finery, had arrived on Coronado.

In his mind's eye, he pictured families strolling along the downtown boulevards, stopping at the elegant old Hotel Del, parents and children, husbands and wives. He pictured himself doing the same, guiding a lovely woman across the grounds of the Del, watching the fireworks as they bloomed in the sky, rejoicing together. With a start, he realized the woman he was imagining himself with was Donna.

He stood gripping the rail, letting the wind beat some sense back into him. He and Donna were working together. That was all. There would be no love connection, no joining of the souls and plans for future Christmases. He'd had that. And it had been taken away. He felt afresh the old ache of loss, as familiar to him as breathing, and he turned his anger toward the dimming sky.

God, why did You take Carrie and leave me?

An image of Donna's tender gaze floated in his heart.

God loves us. He loved Carrie, too, but He had other plans for her.

He wondered, just for a moment, if perhaps God did have plans for him, plans in addition to his rescue swimmer calling. What if those plans included Donna Gallagher?

A darker thought took its place. What if those plans meant he would lose Pauline? Another woman yanked out of his life. Another woman he had not been able to save. He stalked back to his stateroom and splashed water on his face. The image that greeted him in the mirror was stark and he could not ignore the fact that fear shone back at him in the reflection. Though he'd never tell her so, Donna was right. Brent Mitchell, the guy who could leap out of helicopters into the ocean, the hero who would risk his own life on a daily basis, was scared.

He slapped a palm against his reflection so hard it made the glass vibrate. "No more fear. Find your sister. Keep Donna Gallagher safe. End of story." He changed into a nice pair of jeans and a button-up shirt and stowed the bottles of sparkling cider he'd decided to bring in the saddlebags on his motorcycle along with an enormous box of fudge. He wasn't a chocolate guy, but he'd noticed that most of the women he met had a fondness for fudge. A memory of his mother flashed through his mind. Her fudge, with nuts, which required stirring with a long-handled spoon. "Clockwise, Brent," she'd said, though he could never see what difference that could possibly make. She'd made him stand on a chair to do it. He'd never wanted to. There were trees to climb and bikes to race and he'd scurried away at the first opportunity. How he wished now that he hadn't.

He started up the motorcycle and was about to reverse out of his parking place when he saw Jeff Kinsey step out of the bushes. Why here? There was no time to muddle it over.

Kinsey saw him and sprinted through the parking lot. Brent took off after him, quickly closing the gap, pushing the bike as fast as he dared. Jeff scooted through two parked cars and Brent wheeled around, tires squealing. He was nearly to the spot he'd seen Kinsey duck into. Now he was going to get some answers and he wasn't going to hand Kinsey over to Ridley until he got them. He closed the gap; a few feet more.

A woman stepped away from her car right in front of him. One of her arms clutched a full shopping bag and the other the hand of her small son.

Brent jerked to a stop.

The woman shot him a startled look.

Engine idling, heart pounding, he waited for her to cross. As soon as she was safely out of the way, he raced on, stopping to look between the cars and even dismounting to peer underneath. No sign of Kinsey anywhere. Still, Brent edged along slowly, checking every possible hiding place. Nothing. He'd gotten away.

Brent squeezed the grips until his fingers ached. Right there, so close, and he'd let him run off. What was he doing there, anyway? Looking to toss Brent's boat until he found the package Pauline was supposedly going to give him? It undermined his theory that she was in Jeff's custody. If she was alive, why would he still be searching for her package? Pauline was the type who would hand anything over to a needy soul, anyway.

Gut tight, he dutifully called Ridley and filled him in. The officer's responses were clipped and terse. No surprise there. As he disconnected, he got an email with a message reminding him to report in for a preliminary medical check Monday morning. He felt the twin pangs of longing to get back to his job and worry about Pauline's whereabouts.

Setting the thoughts aside, he drove to the address Donna had given him. He arrived at a small well-tended condo set back from a square of immaculately cared-for lawn. Candace had made an effort, hanging glass orna-

ments from a stubby palm in her front yard and a berib-
boned wreath on the door.

He retrieved his offerings and knocked.

JeanBeth opened the door. "Come on in," she said after
giving him a hug. "Angela and Candace are busy wrestling
with the turkey. At the moment, the poultry is winning."

Candace waved from her spot behind the kitchen counter. "The thing's been cooking for hours," she said, pushing the hair back from her pink cheeks. "It's gotta be done
sometime."

"That's the spirit," Angela said. "Let's get this bad boy
back in the oven."

Donna entered through the back sliding door and his
heart gave a little lurch. She wore a soft green sweater and
her hair was caught up in a bundle at the back of her neck.
Luminous was the word that formed in his mind.

"Hey," he croaked.

"Hey," she said. "I just put Radar in the backyard. He's
doing some reconnoitering. As soon as Tracy meets him,
he's not going to have a moment's rest."

"Somehow I don't think he'll mind," Brent said. He offered the bottles of cider and the fudge. "A little Christmas
cheer for the Gallagher family."

"How thoughtful," JeanBeth said. "Our own personal
Santa."

"Ho, ho, ho," he said in his best Santa impersonation.

Childish footsteps pounded down the stairs. "It's
Grampy," cried a little girl with curly hair and freckled
cheeks. "I knew he would come." She bounded into the
room and looked around. "Where's Grampy?"

Brent saw from the horrified look on Donna's face that
he had done something wrong. Very wrong.

"Tracy," Candace said, putting down her pot holders
and coming out to meet her daughter. "Baby, remember,

we talked about that. Grampy…" She cleared her throat. "Grampy died, honey. He's in Heaven now."

The little girl looked at the floor. "With Daddy?"

A lancing pain struck at him at the look on her face. He stood frozen to the spot.

"Yes, Tracy. With Daddy," Candace said through tears that she did not bother to wipe away.

Tracy still did not look up. Abruptly, she tore out of her mother's embrace and ran back up the stairs.

Brent scanned the room. Angela's mouth was drawn in a tight line and JeanBeth stood with her hands over her heart, as if she was holding the child in an invisible embrace.

"I…" Brent started. "Did I say something wrong?"

Donna shook her head. "No. No, not at all. It's just that, uh, my father used to burst through the door every Christmas with an armful of toys, hollering 'Ho, ho, ho.'"

His stomach fell. "She thought I was her grandpa."

Donna nodded miserably. "She doesn't understand yet that he's not coming back."

Candace stood, arms folded around her middle. "I told her. Explained it. I thought she understood."

Brent's stomach dropped to his boots. "I'm really, really sorry."

Donna took his hand. "There's no way you could have known about that tradition. Tracy is confused right now. Please don't blame yourself."

Brent took his keys out. "I should go. Will you tell her I'm sorry?"

"Don't leave," Donna pleaded. "We have to get through this. There has to be a first Christmas without Grampy."

Just as there was a first Christmas without Carrie and without Tracy's father. Tracy was barely two when her father was killed in action, according to Donna, so it probably would not impact her as much as the death of her beloved grandpa.

JeanBeth took a deep breath. "I'll go talk to her."

"I'll do it, Mom," Candace said.

"No." The word came out loud and sharp. JeanBeth took a breath. "No one can understand the way she feels better than I. We'll cry together for a while, and then we'll pray." Her eyes shone with tears. She pointed a finger at Brent. "Don't you leave, sir, and that's an order. We need you." And then she marched up the stairs.

Brent watched the sisters carefully, perplexed. He'd been given orders by the senior officer, but he still felt lower than pond scum for upsetting Tracy. Ruining a kid's Christmas? How could he be forgiven for that? Angela and Candace both offered shaky smiles.

"Mom's directives notwithstanding," Angela said, "we would like it if you stayed."

His eyes found Donna's. Her vote weighed more than any other and he stepped close to her. "It doesn't feel right for me to stay."

She pressed a palm to his chest. "I'm so sorry that happened," she whispered. "But please don't leave, Brent."

Part of his brain vaguely registered that it was not in his power to deny her anything. "Yes," he found himself saying. "Okay."

"I'm sorry, Brent," Candace said as she pressed a glass of cider into his hand. Her face was pale, but she had pulled herself together, another tough Gallagher woman. The kitchen timer dinged. "There will be appetizers at some point, I hope, if those pigs in blankets didn't just incinerate." She bustled back to the kitchen. He heard her whispering with Angela.

"This just can't set her back again," Candace said. Then he heard them praying.

Donna leaned close, hair tickling his cheek. "Tracy had trouble when her father died. She had a bout of selective mutism. Have you heard of that?"

He nodded. "They don't talk?"

"Yes. Candace..." Her voice was a whisper now. "She had to be hospitalized for a while due to the stress and Tracy stopped talking then. It lasted almost a year."

"I can't believe I did that stupid 'ho, ho, ho,' thing. I feel terrible."

She cupped a hand to his cheek. "Don't. These are the things we've got to experience right now. And I'm glad you're here to walk through it with us."

He took her hand and slid her palm to his mouth, pressing a kiss there, feeling his own pulse thumping hard in his throat. "I might just be making it all worse, but if you want me to stay, I will."

A sweet smile curved her lips. "I want you to stay. We all do."

In spite of her assurance, part of him still longed to sprint for the door. In five minutes, he'd managed to make a kid think her grandpa was still alive and watch her fall apart when she learned he wasn't. That had to be some kind of record.

Donna guided him to a table in the corner next to a bookcase. "If we start putting this gingerbread house together, I'm sure Tracy will come over to investigate." She didn't look very sure as she thrust a tube of frosting into his free hand. "How are you with construction plans?"

"I'm a certified genius."

She laughed. "I suppose some extra confidence won't hurt."

They tackled the pieces; she held while he glued. Each minute spent pressed shoulder to shoulder with her seemed to ease the tension from his body. Though his heart ached for Tracy, something about being near Donna soothed him. By the time the structure was standing, Tracy had returned with tearstained cheeks, holding her grandmother's hand, watching the proceedings.

"This is Mr. Mitchell," Donna said. "He's come to help us with the gingerbread house."

"You can call me Brent," he said, holding the tube out to her. "Want to take over?"

She stayed silent, hiding her face against her grandmother's leg. JeanBeth settled into a card chair and hoisted Tracy onto her lap. "We'll just watch for a while."

Brent glued dutifully, keeping Tracy in his peripheral vision. When they got to the fun part, sticking on the candy, he saw Tracy's interest pique as she tried to peer into the paper bags to see what types of candy they contained.

"I'm going to go outside and play with Radar for a while." He left the tube of frosting at the edge of the table near Tracy and let himself out into the backyard. As he did, he saw Tracy approaching the table.

There was a flurry of activity as Angela grabbed her phone and began to take pictures of Tracy and Donna decorating the house. He breathed a sigh. At least something was going right for the kid. As many losses as she'd suffered, she was blessed to have three aunties and a grandma to help her through it. *Blessed?* Had he really come up with that word by himself?

Radar was busily investigating the tangle of bushes along the whitewashed fence. When Brent stepped out, he stopped his sniffing, racing over to bask in a good tummy scratch. Brent picked up a tennis ball from the bucket he figured Donna had brought and lobbed it toward the fence. Radar took off, pouncing on the ball and immediately sitting down to maul it.

"Bring it back, you slacker," he yelled.

Radar eyed him complacently and continued his slobbery work.

Brent tried with two more balls and no better success. Radar now had three tennis balls between his front paws and he alternated between licking them and fussing over them like a mother hen over her chicks.

"Why doesn't he bring 'em back?" came a small voice at his elbow.

Brent whipped around. Tracy was there. Donna watched from the porch.

"I don't know." Brent took a knee, careful not to crowd the child. "He's my sister's dog. She's been trying to teach him to fetch for years, but he just won't do it."

"You should tell your sister he doesn't want to."

"I think you're right." He swallowed. "I'll tell her when I see her."

"Okay."

Tracy looked as though she wanted to play with Radar, but instead she edged back toward the house.

A sudden inspiration occurred to him. Brent took three balls from the bucket. "Maybe I should teach him this instead." He began to juggle the balls.

Tracy's mouth fell open and her face split into a smile. "I wish I could do that."

"I can teach you sometime, if you want."

She cocked her head, and he wondered if he had said something wrong again, tried too hard. The scary man trying to befriend a child he'd upset.

"Okay," she said finally. "Can I play with the dog?"

"Sure. His name is Radar, but don't expect him to bring back any tennis balls."

Tracy scampered off to pet Radar, who was happy to leave his ball collection to play with her. Donna moved to his side. "Where'd you learn to juggle?"

"My dad. I started with scarves and worked my way up to pineapples. I'm very entertaining at parties. You should see what I can do with bowling pins."

"I can imagine."

There were so many worries circling around in his head,

whirling around like the juggled balls. He knew he should tell her about the encounter with Jeff Kinsey at his boat, but he was distracted as the emerging moonlight caught her hair. Inside, strains of off-key Christmas carols started up and he heard JeanBeth laugh. Tracy squealed as Radar licked her chin. Donna watched her niece with a look of inexpressible tenderness. *Later*, he told himself. *Let her have her moment of Christmas joy.*

He realized that a tiny flicker of that feeling was bouncing around in his heart, too.

Christmas joy. His sister would be proud, if she were only there to see it. Swallowing against a thickening in his throat, he followed Donna back inside.

They squeezed around the tiny table, eating a turkey that was only a little too dry and enjoying plenty of cider and conversation. The gingerbread house was a triumph, at least in Tracy's eyes, and that was really all that mattered, Donna thought. Tracy did not seem to mind that it leaned a bit on the starboard side. Each tradition forced bittersweet emotions to the surface. Dad was not there to carve the turkey or offer a sparkling-cider toast or swing Tracy up on his shoulders so she could touch the tippy-top of the Christmas tree. Wrapped in each tradition was heartache and loss, and the evening produced many tears. Along with the anguish, there were clasped hands, fierce hugs, unskilled singing and blobs of whipped cream on hot cocoa. Somehow they staggered through and Donna's emotions had run the gamut by the time nine o'clock rolled around.

With Donna manning the sink and Brent the dishtowel, the holiday mess was soon cleared away. She craved a moment of quiet to soothe her frazzled nerves, so she stepped outside, breathing in the clean Coronado air. The cloud-draped sky promised a storm coming, which lent a chill to the air. The weather reports predicted it would be a big one. Leaves rattled in the palms and rippled through the thick hedge of shrubs that framed the yard.

Radar, exhausted from playing with Tracy, lay with his head on his big paws, resting.

Donna sighed, reaching out for a chair when a gleam of white caught her attention. Something in the shrubs. She walked closer to investigate when Radar suddenly shot to his feet barking and charged past her toward the bushes. The white gleam came into focus. Jeff Kinsey's face. She screamed.

SIXTEEN

Kinsey grabbed her arm and started to drag her to the side gate. Radar barked and lunged. Donna tried to break Kinsey's hold, but his fingers dug into the tendons of her wrist. She kicked out and got him in the side of the shin, but he held on. Dropping to her knees, she hoped the dead weight would slow him as she continued to scream.

He hauled her toward the gate, kicking out at Radar, who grabbed at his sleeve and tugged with all his might. Their efforts slowed him for just long enough. Brent exploded out the back door and hurled himself on top of Jeff.

Jeff went down hard on the grass. They rolled around, grappling for a hold until Brent emerged victorious, rolling Jeff onto his stomach and kneeling between his shoulder blades.

"Get off," Jeff wheezed.

"No way."

Angela raced over to them.

"Get me a rope or duct tape," Brent called to her. He looked at Donna. "Are you hurt?"

Her shoulder throbbed and she rubbed at it. "No, rattled, is all."

Candace joined them and her face went slack with dismay. "I'm going to go sit with Tracy. She's not asleep yet and I don't want her to come outside and find this. I'll call the police."

"Give me a minute," Brent said. She looked at him questioningly.

Brent's eyes caught hers. "Time is running out for my sister. I want to ask him some questions. I may never get the chance again."

Candace hesitated on the button. Her eyes shifted to her mother and sisters, asking the silent question. Was Brent Mitchell a man to be trusted? The seconds ticked by before she answered. "Okay. Five minutes, then I call."

Brent nodded. He looked at Donna. "Are you sure you aren't hurt?"

A couple of slow stretches eased the pain in her shoulder. "I'm okay." She clipped Radar onto the leash she'd left on the table and secured him.

Brent hauled Jeff to his feet and planted him in a patio chair, then bound his hands and feet with duct tape. Jeff's eyes were wide, lips wet with saliva. He coughed violently. Donna couldn't help thinking the man was ill.

"What are you gonna do to me?" he panted.

Brent sat opposite him. "That's not the way this is going to go. You are going to answer questions, not ask them."

Jeff's mouth tightened and he went quiet.

"Where is my sister?"

He chewed his lip and rocked slightly in the chair, breathing rapidly.

"Where is she?" Brent said.

"I don't know." He coughed some more.

"You're lying. You've been following me and Donna, trying to find some money my sister left. You took her car. You know where she is." He forced out the words. "Did you kill her?"

Jeff squirmed in the chair. "Pauline was good to me. I'd never hurt her. She tried to help me get clean, got me a job. When I got into trouble, she even went to the private eye for help."

"My father." Donna gasped. "What trouble?"

He sucked in a breath. "I took some money."

"From Darius Fields?"

Jeff's eyes went round with fear. "Got beat up. Then he burned up my trailer."

"Darius did?"

Jeff clamped his mouth closed. "Cops wouldn't believe me. Pauline went to the private eye to see if he could dig up some proof. That trailer was all I had, man."

"What did you do to my sister?" Brent asked, voice coming close to a shout.

"Nothing, I told you. She was my friend. Went to meet her on the beach. She was gonna give me a plane ticket and some cash to lie low for a while. We saw Darius's car coming. She gave me her keys and I waited in the car, but it took too long." He coughed, doubling over. "Took way too long and when I looked…" He sobbed. "I'll never forget that rainbow scarf she was wearing."

"What?" Brent demanded. "What happened?"

He cried, tears dripping off his unshaven chin. "After it happened, I didn't know what to do. I waited a long time at the beach. Radar was running around, whining and barking and stuff. I couldn't leave him there. I took him and left him at Open Vistas. I figured Harvey would take care of him. Later I left her car behind some sporting-goods store."

Brent was nearly wild now. "What happened to my sister, Jeff? You need to tell me right now."

He rocked back and forth. "I didn't hurt her."

"You're a liar, trying to blame it on Darius. All you are concerned about is your next fix."

"I know, okay?" he shouted. "I know. I'm a loser and a mess-up and I've lost everything I ever had. The only person who still believed I was worth anything was Pauline and I didn't hurt her."

"Then who did?" Brent leaned closer. "What did you see on the beach, Jeff? You've got to tell me."

Donna watched the fear flicker up again. "You're afraid of Darius. He did something to Pauline and you are afraid to finger him because he beat you up and burned your trailer. He found out my father was investigating him."

More coughing.

"You're not innocent in all this, are you?" Brent snapped. "Maybe you're in it with Darius. Working with him somehow. You caused Bruce's accident because you were covering for Darius, following orders."

Jeff's eyes cleared for a moment. "I didn't. I don't even have a set of wheels."

"Your vehicle was the one that forced Bruce Gallagher's car off the road. You killed him and injured Sarah Gallagher."

Jeff's eyes popped. "No," he screamed. "I haven't driven that truck in months. Don't have the money for gas or insurance, so I left it at the campground. Was gonna get it later." He began to cry. "Aww, man."

Brent knelt to try to catch Jeff's eye, but the man would not meet his gaze. "Jeff," he said softly, "you're right. My sister was the only one who believed in you, thought you were worth something, so tell me straight, for her sake. What happened to Pauline? What went down on the beach that day?"

Jeff curled up, head bent low, and began to moan. His sobs turned into gasps for air as his eyes rolled back in his head and he went unconscious.

The night was a blur. Donna watched through a fog of confusion as Jeff Kinsey was put under arrest and transported by ambulance to the hospital. Brent stayed with the Gallaghers until late into the evening talking it over, twisting and turning the tidbits every which way until they were about to go nuts with it. The two questions stubbornly refused to be answered.

Had Kinsey driven Bruce Gallagher and Sarah off the road?

Where was Pauline?

She knew Kinsey's words were tormenting Brent. *That*

rainbow scarf... I waited a long time... Brent pulled himself out of the chair just before eleven when there was a heavy knock on the door.

Donna was thrilled to see Marco on the doorstep. He dropped his duffel bag on the floor and greeted each woman with a fierce hug. It might have been Donna's imagination, but she thought Marco's embrace of Candace lasted a bit longer, his big hands clasping her tightly around the waist as she pressed a kiss to his cheek.

He flicked a glance at Brent, eyes narrowing. "What are you doing here, Coastie?"

"He's been chasing bad guys out of our backyard," Jean-Beth said. "So stop glowering."

Marco's frown deepened, anyway. JeanBeth made him sit and poured him some coffee. "How was your trip?" she said, her voice gentle.

He blinked, shifted in his chair, the mug of coffee small in his big hands. "Done. Let's talk about the case."

Angela spelled it out with precise detail from the day Marco left to Jeff Kinsey's bizarre confession in the backyard before he was arrested. Marco sat quietly, taking it all in.

"So what's your gut say, Coastie?"

"I think Kinsey is telling the truth about most of it. Darius Fields is behind whatever happened to Pauline and Bruce."

Marco drank some coffee.

"Well?" Brent demanded. "What's your sage opinion?"

Another swallow. "You're wrong."

"Wrong?"

"Kinsey's an addict. You can't trust an addict. Most likely he's the guy."

"You haven't even been here and you've got the case solved in ten minutes?" Brent said.

Marco was implacable. "His car was put at the accident

scene. He's been at Pauline's house, your boat, the Gallagher home. Every turn, he's there."

"He fingered Darius."

Marco shrugged. "The word of an addict against the word of a gambler."

"He must be telling the truth about taking Radar to Open Vistas. The dog couldn't get there by himself."

"That part might be true, but addicts are liars. Period. He wanted money for drugs and he's desperate. That's the only truthful part of his story."

"All right," Brent said. "You've got it all figured out. What do you think happened?"

"Pauline was helping Kinsey. Promised him money. He got impatient. Things went bad."

"Why cause the crash, then?" Donna said.

"The kid knew she went to Bruce, probably because she had fears he would hurt her. Kinsey was starting to make demands, frighten her, and she wanted someone to keep an eye on him. Bruce nosed around, asking questions when Pauline didn't show up to their meeting. Kinsey needed to stop those questions or he'd be fingered for her disappearance."

Brent got to his feet. "So, bottom-line it for me, Marco."

Marco stayed silent.

Donna felt a thrill of dread.

"Go ahead," Brent said. "You've gone this far. Say it."

"I'm sorry, man, but the most likely scenario is that your sister is dead." Though the words were hard, Marco's face was soft with compassion. "Kinsey killed her on the beach, took her in the car and…" He cleared his throat. "Like I said, I'm sorry but I know if it was me, I'd want someone to tell me straight."

The room fell so quiet that Donna could hear the sound of water dripping from the kitchen faucet. They had probably all thought the same thing about Pauline's fate many times, but to hear it stated so baldly cut deep. Brent did not flinch. Instead, he grabbed his coat.

"Thank you for having me this evening, ladies. I appreciate your hospitality." Then he was out the front door.

Donna ran after him. Patters of rain dappled her face.

"Wait, Brent," she called.

He did not slow. He got on his motorcycle and revved the engine, then reached for his helmet.

"Brent," she said again. "I'm sorry. That was terrible to hear. Marco has a lot of great qualities, but tact isn't one of them."

His face was stony, shoulders stiff. "It's what you've all been thinking, anyway," he said. "Right? What everyone in that room thinks?"

She could not lie. Instead, she gripped his biceps. "There's still room for hope."

"That's what I tell myself, but I've always preferred action to hope."

"What are you going to do?"

He shook his head. "Don't know yet."

"I'm praying that we find Pauline safe and sound."

He looked away for a moment. "I'd better go. It's late."

"Let's talk tomorrow. We can figure out what to do next."

He shook his head. "You've got Marco here. He'll know exactly how to proceed with the investigation about your father, I'm sure."

Her stomach dropped. "We're still a team until it's finished. Aren't we?"

His glance drifted to the door. "Your team is in there, Donna."

No, she wanted to say. *I want you by my side, and not just to dig out answers*, she realized. But that wasn't how he was seeing things. They were working partners only. And now he'd been replaced. Investigators who were no longer on the case together. Why had she allowed herself to feel anything else? So much for good sense. So much for the lessons learned from Nate.

"Will you be okay?"

His smile was forced. "Of course. Take care of Radar for me, will you? Until I can figure something out?"

Not trusting herself to speak, she nodded.

He gave her a last long look and drove away.

SEVENTEEN

Brent reported for his medical checkup Monday morning as required. He'd taken Sunday to stew. He'd run five miles before dawn and practically worn a path pacing the dock, and nothing soothed the current of worry that was fluxing into outright fear.

Fear. He detested the feeling. It brought him back to the violent shock of the plane hitting the water, the jerk of the rescuer pulling him clear, Carrie's last cry before they struck the ocean. The darkness filled him until it pushed the prayer from his lips.

Help me.

It tempered the horror. He did not understand why, but just saying it, offering it to God, relieved the tension. He wished he could ask Donna about it, but she was better off without him. If Marco was right, Ridley would have the truth out of Kinsey soon enough and the Gallaghers' case would be closed. Would Kinsey also reveal what he'd done to his sister? Nothing would ever be resolved in his life until he knew what had happened to Pauline.

Help me.

The prayer still circulated inside him, but being back on the base renewed the fire he always felt. Now it seemed even more intense. *Do the job. So others may live.* While he was on duty, he'd have to trust Ridley to find Pauline. As much as it grated on his nerves, for the moment, it was his only choice.

"You're cleared as far as your physical condition," the doctor said.

"What does that mean?"

The doctor hesitated. "The situation with your sister. Very difficult."

"It won't interfere with my doing my duties, Doc."

"How could it not?"

"Because when we're called up, I'm 100 percent there and you know it. Ask my crew—they'll vouch for me."

"I have no doubt." He cocked his head. "But I'm concerned you've got a huge mental strain right now."

"Fair enough," Brent said, pulling on his shirt. "Be concerned, but don't ground me."

There was an endless moment. Brent gritted his teeth, stood ramrod straight and waited.

"All right," the doctor said. "You're cleared for your shift tomorrow."

Brent held himself to a professional nod, though he felt like letting out a whoop. One aspect of his life, his reason for getting through each day, had been given back to him. Tomorrow he would report for his twenty-four-hour shift. His body itched for action, but even if there wasn't a search-and-rescue call, he'd be back with his crew where he belonged. It was the only thing he had to hold on to, since he'd walked away from Donna.

Back on his bike, he thought of her, the laughter they had shared the night before, the ease with which he could talk to her. She'd come closer to him than any woman ever had besides Carrie, until Kinsey's arrest changed everything.

He knew Ridley wouldn't tell him much until the interrogations were complete, and Marco would be in the office with the Gallagher sisters, working on tying up the case as best they could.

But what about Darius? And Fran? Brent could not get the feeling out of his gut that there was some truth in Kinsey's accusation. The image of those pink roses intruded on his thoughts no matter how he resisted. All the evidence pointed to Jeff Kinsey, just as Marco said. What would it hurt to snoop around? He had a whole day to kill, anyway, and at least it made him feel as if he was still doing something for Pauline.

He was about to head for Darius's shop in Mission Bay when his phone trilled.

It was a call from Donna. She sounded breathless. His nerves jangled.

"I heard from Ridley this morning. The doctors say Kinsey's got pneumonia and he's been admitted at the hospital. He's too weak to talk right now."

He groaned. Another delay.

Donna went on, her voice an excited whisper. "I'm here now checking in to visit Sarah, and guess who just showed up."

"Darius?"

"Fran. She's got a bunch of flowers with her. She asked what room Jeff Kinsey was in, but the desk clerk wouldn't tell her. Odd, right? She's on her phone right now, texting."

"Yeah, odd." The skin along his neck tingled. "Keep an eye on her if you can. I'll be there in ten minutes."

As he drove, he tried to figure out what Fran's interest in Jeff Kinsey might possibly be.

Could be she'd struck up a friendship with him when he worked for Darius.

A friendship? With a guy whom her fiancé would happily murder?

Right, he thought as he increased speed.

The lobby was a swarm of activity as a group of carolers wearing Santa hats arrived. As they arranged themselves and sang with gusto, Donna lost track of Fran in the milling crowd. Ten minutes later she spotted the woman stepping off the elevator, which was on its way down. Donna lingered in the lobby, keeping to the side of the tinsel-covered Christmas tree to prevent Fran from seeing her.

She watched through the sliding doors as Fran exited the hospital. After she sniffed the bouquet of carnations, touching her cheek to the satin petals, she dumped it into the trash, got into her car and left.

Donna had no idea what to make of it. As she waited for Brent, she dialed the office. Candace answered. "Marco's on the other line. What's up?"

"Can you have Marco use his connections to find out anything he can about Fran Mercer?"

"I thought we'd decided that wasn't the right trail to follow."

"There's something going on, Candace. Trust me on this, okay?"

There was a pause. She imagined her sister's thoughts. *You're not an investigator. You don't know what you're doing. You're grasping at straws because you have feelings for Brent.* She clenched the phone.

"Okay," she said. "But promise me you aren't going to do anything dangerous."

"I promise," she agreed with a sigh of relief.

They said goodbye. For a moment after the disconnection, she savored the feeling. She and her sister had endured their share of hostility, anger and out-and-out fighting, but Candace trusted her and it buoyed her spirits. She was grateful to God that He had softened both their hearts with forgiveness. *Sisters are with you cradle to grave,* her grandmother used to say. What finer blessing could there be?

With renewed fire, she determined to head back up to the second and third floors and check things out for herself. She'd made it to the elevator when Brent caught up. He moved with the grace of a tiger, big strides eating up the ground.

He squeezed through the doors before they closed.

"We've got to stop meeting in elevators," he said.

"You look happier than when I last saw you."

"Got the all clear to return to duty tomorrow."

"Oh. I'm happy for you." And she was, mostly, though heaviness tugged at her insides. His life, his purpose. Without her.

He smiled and urged her to fill him in.

"I've only seen a woman throw away flowers once," he said once she was finished.

She raised an eyebrow. "Care to elaborate?"

He flushed. "Uh, no, but suffice it to say, I had it coming. Fran's up to something. Those flowers were just a prop. I figured I'd do a little sleuthing, start at the third floor and work my way down."

They stepped out on the third floor.

"There's Kinsey's room," Brent said. A Coronado cop was stationed outside his door, thumbs hooked through his belt loops. "Glad Ridley's not taking any chances."

Donna felt better. Certainly Fran had not been admitted to see Kinsey.

"I'm going to see if I can charm my way past the cop," Brent said.

Donna watched as Brent put on an easy smile and approached the officer. He was ordered to stop before he got halfway there.

"No visitors, sir. Turn around and go back, please."

Brent held up his palms. "I understand. I just wanted to check on Kinsey's condition. He's involved in my sister's disappearance—I'm sure Officer Ridley has told you."

"Yes, sir. He told me under no circumstances is anyone other than medical personnel to pass through this door, especially an individual named Brent Mitchell or anyone with the last name of Gallagher."

Donna almost smiled.

Brent grudgingly thanked the officer and turned around.

"That went well," she said.

"Should have had you try it. You're way better-looking."

She laughed. "At least we know Fran didn't get in to see him, either."

A swell of noise announced the arrival of the Christmas carolers, Santa hats and grins in place. They started in on the singing. Nurses and visitors stepped out into the hallway to listen and the space was soon crammed with people. Donna made her way to the far end of the floor.

"Sarah," Donna said, knocking softly to wake her sister. Sarah opened one eye. "What is that racket?"

"It's caroling," she said. "Do you want to get in the wheelchair and go listen?"

"No," she said, closing her eyes.

Donna did not miss the pain that rippled across her sister's face. Not the physical kind, but the reminder that the season was filled with anguish where there used to be joy, anguish for which Sarah blamed herself.

She pressed a kiss to her sister's temple and walked back out into the hallway and over to the far end. Brent leaned against the wall, alert, as the carolers swarmed around him. Donna noticed the door to the stairwell open. A man with overalls and a cap pulled down over his eyes stepped out. He carried a metal bucket. Brent stiffened. The singing rose in volume, loud in the narrow hallway.

The cop stood in the doorway, not budging from his post.

Donna lost sight of the man in overalls for a moment as the Santa hats filled the corridor. Then, as if in slow motion, she saw him take something from the bucket and lob it into the air. It exploded with a deafening boom and a brilliant flash of light.

Brent scrambled toward the explosion, his body clumsy from the disabling noise, blinded by the flash. When his vision cleared after a long five seconds of furious blinking, he saw that the cop had been knocked backward into the wall and lay unmoving on the floor. Brent plunged toward him, but he could not make progress against the screaming carolers.

"Fire!" a voice to his left shouted.

The smell of smoke burned his nose. Flames erupted as a cart full of paper products caught fire.

A nurse picked herself up from the floor and leaped into action, activating a fire alarm and assisting those nearest her who had fallen. Brent batted the burning towels away from the others before they could catch flame. Donna appeared with a fire extinguisher she'd taken from the wall, but the panicked carolers prevented her from getting through.

"Catch," she called, tossing him the extinguisher. He snagged it.

"Give it to me," an orderly commanded, and Brent was happy to oblige.

He struggled to see over the madness and when he did, his breath froze in his lungs. Kinsey, clad in a hospital gown, face blank, was staggering toward the stairwell, an IV tube trailing from his arm.

"Stop," Brent thundered over the cacophony. Kinsey did not look up, pushing through the stairwell door. The workman with the cap hustled after him, stepping over the prostrate police officer. The workman didn't look back, just hurried after Kinsey.

Was it Darius? The figure seemed too bulky. Brent hastily helped a woman to her feet, steadied another and reached Donna, who was assisting those nearest to her. His ears still throbbed from the bang, which had probably exceeded 170 decibels.

"What was that?" Donna panted.

"Stun grenade. It's meant to disorient."

"It works," she said, shaking her head. "My senses are scrambled."

"Kinsey's getting away. Call Ridley."

"Sarah's already done it."

He made for the stairs, but as much as he wanted to pursue the two men, he could not leave the downed officer. After he did a quick assessment, he shouted to a nearby nurse. "Here." He pointed to the injured cop. "He's breathing on his own. Pulse is steady."

She nodded, immediately taking charge of the victim.

Two hospital security people emerged through the far door and began trying to restore order. An elderly woman with her glasses knocked askew pawed at Brent's arm. "What should we do? What's happened?"

Squeezing her hand, he helped her to a chair and waved over a doctor who was jogging toward the confusion. "It's going to be okay, ma'am. Just sit here for a minute and catch your breath."

Brent finally extricated himself from the carolers and sprinted for the stairwell. Donna followed.

Throwing the door open, he could hear the escapees. When he risked a quick look over the rail, the man with the cap had grabbed Kinsey by the shoulders, leading him down the stairwell. Kinsey was weak, stumbling. Was he abducting Kinsey or helping him escape? It was impossible to tell, but Brent wasn't going to let him get away in any case. He increased speed and made it to the final landing just as the two were a couple of steps from the door to the outside.

The workman had now picked Kinsey up and slung him over his shoulder. Brent came close enough to get a good look. It was Mooch, the guy who had tried to run Darius down in the ocean.

"You're not getting out of here," Brent shouted. "Give it up."

"I'm never gonna be caught by you, Boy Wonder."

Yeah? Just watch. As Brent attacked the final flight of stairs, his foot tangled with Donna's as she sprinted to catch up. He stumbled, catching himself on the railing. Momentum carried Donna forward before he could stop her. Her hair was tangled, her face resolute; his brain noted how very beautiful she was as his gut tightened in fear.

"Bye, bye, Boy Wonder," he heard Mooch say.

"Donna, stop," he yelled.

As he got to his feet again, the stairwell seemed to explode. He watched Donna, framed by an intense ball of light, somersaulting through the air. Then his senses went black.

EIGHTEEN

Donna felt as though she was being smothered by the darkness and silence. She must have landed in the bottom of some cold, dark well where her senses would not cooperate. Then came the noise and the sensation of tumbling.

At the edges of her consciousness there was heat and the beginnings of pain.

In her daze she realized she was being carried, lowered to the ground and rolled until the breath was squeezed out of her.

Stop, she wanted to cry to her torturer, but her mouth would not cooperate.

Finally, the movement subsided. She realized she was outside, lying on the grass. Through her blurred vision, she made out Brent's face, lined with terror. His mouth was moving, but she could not hear him. She wanted to reach up, to stroke his troubled brow and reassure him, but her arms were leaden, trapped at her sides.

Her ears began to clear.

"Donna," he was whispering. "Say something to me. Please."

"I'm dizzy."

The two words seemed to break the horror that held him captive. He leaned in and gently pressed his forehead to hers. "Honey, you scared me." His breath was warm and comforting on her face.

She wanted to tip up her chin the tiniest bit and give him a reassuring kiss, but he was busy scanning her body, feeling her pulse, calling to someone who approached them.

"Kinsey…?"

"He's gone. Doesn't matter. Cops will get him. Lie still, okay? Until we have you checked out."

She struggled to a sitting position in spite of his protests. "It was another of those flash grenades?"

He nodded.

"I hate those things."

"Me, too. It threw you off your feet and your clothes caught fire."

She looked down at her blackened pants. "Is that why you were tossing me all over the grass?"

"Yes. I think you may have some burns and you fell hard against the stairwell. They're going to need to check you for a possible concussion."

She groaned as she started to feel some pain in her arms. "My father always said I had the hardest head of all the Gallagher daughters, but personally, I think Candace should get that title."

He smiled, but his gaze drifted over the parking lot. Approaching sirens whined. She caught up his hand, throat thick. "You let them get away, didn't you, because of me?"

His eyes were dark pools of oil as he looked at the clouded backdrop of the sky. "Ridley will find them. Kinsey's sick. They can't get too far."

"I'm sorry," she said, grasping his hand. "You should have gone after them and left me."

"I couldn't do that." He looked at her, brimming with deep emotion. Was the intensity his commitment to his duty? Or to her? Gently, he brushed her singed hair away from her neck. "You're okay. That's all that matters at the moment."

Her heart beat an exuberant song until she remembered. It was his job to care for the victim. He'd stayed because he was a rescuer who would never leave a patient.

Pain inside dueled with the stinging in her arms and back.

He pressed his lips to her face and stayed there, as if to

reassure himself that she was really okay, until two nurses made it to her side, dropping to their knees to examine her. Donna's efforts to wave them away did no good and she was loaded onto a gurney and wheeled into the hospital, where they painfully cleaned her cuts and abrasions and treated the burns on her upper arms.

She endured a scan to be sure there was no concussion. Her mother, Candace and Angela appeared at her bedside as she waited for a final check-over. Brent hustled in a moment later. Why did her heart surge every time she saw him?

His face told her the news was not good.

"Cops think they made it over the bridge. Mooch was driving the green car. They've got someone going to interview Fran."

JeanBeth shook her head. "Was this Mooch character working with Kinsey?"

Brent shoved a hand through his cropped hair. "I have no idea. Last time I saw him, he was doing his best to run Darius down in the water. Darius owes him money, but I don't see how Kinsey fits in here."

Marco slammed into the room, hands balled into fists. "Happy now, Coastie? You've landed Donna in the hospital and she could have been killed."

"That wasn't—" Donna started, but Brent's eyes flashed black fire at Marco.

"Mooch tossed a flash grenade," Brent said. "Clearly, there's more to this case than you thought."

Marco's jaw clenched. "All I know is, you don't let a girl run after tough guys while you take your sweet time getting down the stairs."

Brent straightened, nose to nose with Marco. "That's not the way it went down."

Donna could see the muscle twitch in Brent's clenched jaw, the same action mirrored in Marco's.

"You've been stirring up this hornet's nest when it should be left to the cops. Kinsey is the guy, just like I told you. There's nothing more to be done than to let them do their jobs and keep this family out of it."

"Would you say that if it was your sister missing?" Brent said.

"I'm saying that because these women are my family and I'm not going to let you put them at risk."

"He didn't cause this situation today, Marco," Donna said.

"Yeah?" Marco's voice dropped and he stared right into Brent's face. "Donna ran right into that flash grenade instead of you. How is that right?"

They stayed riveted there for one long moment.

"Don't blame him," Donna said.

"Don't have to," Marco said. "He already blames himself, don't you, Coastie?"

Brent flinched.

Marco pressed the advantage. "You know you need to leave this family alone. I'm sorry about your sister, man, really, I am, but I need to protect the Gallaghers."

"From me?"

Marco gave one slow nod. "Bruce would want it that way."

Brent's expression wavered. Donna's eyes welled up.

"You know," Brent said softly, "I always thought I was one of the good guys." He cast one more look around, at her mother and Candace, and one lingering glance at Donna before he turned away.

"Brent…" Donna called, but he was already gone.

Donna glared at Marco through misty eyes. "How could you do that, Marco?"

Marco met her glare with maddening calm. "I'll continue to work the leads, look into Fran and Darius, but it's better that none of you are involved."

Better? She felt like yelling. Watching Brent walk away, right out of her life, did not feel the slightest bit better to her. In fact, it felt a lot like having her soul ripped out.

She felt Candace watching her and Donna knew that her sister could sense the truth she did not want to admit. Brent had taken a piece of her heart when he walked out that door. Candace slipped her hand over Donna's, but she yanked it away.

"I'm going to get dressed now. May I have some privacy?"

"The doctors want to admit you," Candace said.

"No. I'm leaving. Now can I have a moment alone?" When they hesitated, she added, "Please?"

They filed out and Donna was grateful that the tears held off until she was alone.

It was a relief to report to the base in San Diego. The sector was still abuzz with the news of the recovery of eight tons of cocaine that would not make its way onto American soil thanks to the intervention of the US Coast Guard. He wanted to enjoy the chatter, but it washed over him, leaving him strangely numb.

He wondered if Donna's burns were hurting, if the police had caught up with Kinsey and Mooch, if anything had been gleaned from Fran Mercer. Worst of all, recriminations rang through his mind with relentless persistence. *Donna ran right into that flash grenade instead of you. Carrie got onto that plane because of you.*

And Pauline? Was she lost forever because he'd bungled things? Three women whom he cared about. More than cared about. Donna's clear blue eyes swam before him.

He cut off the thoughts and focused on the weather reports during his shift briefing. The approaching storm was expected to bring waves of twelve to fourteen feet with potential flooding along the San Diego River. Excitement kicked up in his gut. Bad weather meant the potential for being called up and that was every rescue swimmer's constant craving. Generally, his tasks were more benign, assisting with distressed recreation boaters and surfers who underestimated the power of the ocean, but there was always the potential for a big event that would challenge his skills and push him to the limits.

He reconnected with his crew.

Pilot Bruno "Bear" Philippi clapped him on the back. "Glad to have you back, Brent. Are we gonna see some action tonight, you think?"

"Hope so."

Bear's look lingered a little too long. "I'm hoping things turn out all right for your sister," he said quietly. "The wife and I have been praying."

Mack, the flight mechanic who had delivered Brent safely back to their Jayhawk helicopter more times than he could count, nodded his silent agreement over the top of his coffee cup.

They understood why he answered with a nod. The briefing room was no place to open that can of anguish. Do the job, and save lives. That was the focus and he felt grateful for that.

The SAR alarm sounded just as Brent was helping himself to a cup of coffee. They listened to the brief as they grabbed their gear and jogged to the Jayhawk helicopter through pouring rain. The rotors churned them into the air, the vibrations both ferocious and comforting.

"Boater in distress," the pilot reported, "about two miles out."

It was dark now, rain falling in sheets as they roared over the Pacific.

"What a night for a sail," Mack called over the noise. "Some sort of man-versus-nature test?"

Brent had long ago given up trying to figure out why

people chose to ignore all weather warnings and believe their sailing prowess would help them defeat the ocean. The ocean was a formidable foe, unless you were a rescue swimmer, he thought with pride. Then the odds were more even.

"No casualties tonight," he murmured to himself. "Not on my watch."

Searching for a victim in the open ocean was like trying to find a coconut bobbing on the waves. Most of the time, only the top of a head was visible. Bear circled the helicopter low while he and Mack leaned out the open doors, straining to find any sign below.

"Got it," Brent called. "Boat in the water at your eleven."

The helicopter's powerful nose light, nicknamed the "midnight sun," picked out the outline of an overturned motorboat.

The captain had figured something that size would do the job against the storm-whipped waves? Madness.

"There," Mack called, stabbing a finger at a point in the darkness.

Brent could just make out the flash of white from an arm or shoulder.

"Alive?" the pilot called.

"Unknown," Bear said.

While Brent pulled on his flippers and dive mask, they decided on a direct deployment approach and Mack attached Brent's harness to a cable.

After a thumbs-up from Brent, Mack eased him over the side. "Swimmer away," Brent heard him say as he plunged toward the angry waves.

Wind tore at him as he rappelled down. He swallowed the instant of fear and stoked up the anger instead. If this was the day God was going to take him as He had done with Carrie, Brent wasn't going down without a fight.

Straining to see through the curtains of rain, Brent

could hear Mack's shouted directions to Bear as he strove to keep the Jayhawk in a steady hover.

Brent tried to keep the victim in sight as he hit the water and surfaced just in time for a wave to pick him up and slam him back to the surface. The breath whooshed out of him and for a minute he wondered if his back was broken. He felt the hoist line pull him back upward as Mack probably figured Brent had been injured.

"Stay, stay," he radioed, signaling Mack to leave him in the water.

Fighting the waves, he spotted the victim again and made for the spot, struggling against the water, which seemed determined to yank his quarry away. The sea spray made it impossible to see clearly, but the person was Caucasian, wearing some sort of dress, long hair plastered against her face. Woman in a dress in the ocean during inclement weather?

He reached her, swimming up shouting words of encouragement she probably could not hear. Didn't matter. Big orange helicopter and a guy in a coast guard suit were welcome sights to a drowning victim regardless.

She was limp at first until Brent reached out. Suddenly the head jerked up and Brent almost lost his hold. It wasn't a woman. It was Jeff Kinsey, still in his hospital gown.

NINETEEN

When Brent reached for him, terror took over and Kinsey lunged, flailing and grabbing at Brent, knocking his swimmer's mask off. Kinsey found some reserve of strength and clung to Brent with amazing tenacity. Brent jerked free, then used his momentum to flip Kinsey and grab him around the neck. Still fighting against Kinsey's thrashing, Brent managed to get the rescue strop around him and give a thumbs-up to Mack, who began the delicate task of hoisting them up against the raging wind.

As they rose, Brent's mind whirled. Kinsey. Attempting an escape to Mexico maybe? Did he really think he would make it, sick as he was, without even proper clothing? But then, drug addicts weren't always able to think through their actions. If he had been a moment later, Kinsey would certainly have drowned. Brent clutched him tighter. He'd saved a life, though it was the life of a man who had most likely taken his sister's.

He clung to Kinsey until Mack eased the victim into the chopper. Brent followed, took off his harness and knelt next to Kinsey, whose eyes were slowly closing.

"Stay awake, Kinsey," Brent said.

"You know him?" Mack said, eyes wide with surprise.

"He's the guy who the cops think took my sister."

Mack's mouth fell open. "What?"

Brent felt for Kinsey's pulse, which was faint. He rubbed two knuckles along Kinsey's sternum, a technique to cause enough discomfort to rouse the patient. Kinsey came to, his limbs thrashing.

"Stay still. You're safe now," Brent said. The sudden

movement could propel the cold blood in his limbs back into his heart and cause cardiac arrest.

Kinsey stopped moving, his eyes swiveling to Brent.

"I can't believe it's you that got me out," he whispered.

"Me neither."

"If you had known it was me…" he whispered, "would you still have jumped in?"

Would he? Would he have dived into that water to rescue the man who had most likely murdered Pauline? "Yes," he said.

Kinsey frowned in concentration. "Why?"

"Because it's what I do."

"Save people who don't deserve it?"

"Yeah, and people who do."

He smiled, his face ghostly pale. "My mother used to say that's called grace, getting something you don't deserve."

"Please," Brent said gently. "Tell me what you did to my sister."

Kinsey's smile vanished. "Pauline was a one-of-a-kind lady. I didn't deserve her friendship."

"Tell me," he pleaded. "Just say it."

He could feel Mack's bewilderment beside him.

"I'm sorry," Kinsey whispered, just before he stopped breathing.

Donna drove to the Glorietta Bay Marina the next evening. She had no plan, only the need to see Brent since he'd finished his twenty-four-hour shift, to hear from his mouth how he was coping. Marco had broken the news to her about how Brent had rescued Jeff Kinsey only to have Kinsey die en route to the hospital. She stood there at the black security fence, rain drizzling against her umbrella, her jacket aggravating the burns on her arms.

Ridley believed that Kinsey had struck a deal somehow with Mooch to help him escape, but Donna found it hard to believe. So many pieces still did not fit. Why had Fran shown up at the hospital with flowers? In her story to the police, she'd claimed she'd felt sorry for Kinsey, the desperate kid who had worked for her fiancé for a brief while, and wanted to wish him well when she'd heard he'd been hospitalized.

Donna wasn't convinced. Marco and her sisters weren't, either, and she knew they were working together to see if they could find some evidence that Fran and Darius were involved. If only her father was still alive, he'd tell them exactly how to proceed. Grief surged through her as she clung to the bars with one hand. She desperately wanted to text Brent or call him, something, but she knew it was not right to bother a man who had clearly tried to separate himself.

She stared through the fence, kicking herself for coming. There was nothing she could do here. She whispered a prayer to the wind and turned back to the cement path to find Brent standing there, rain beading against his leather jacket and the brim of his coast guard cap.

"Hi," she said. "I, um, was in the area and I came to see if you were all right. Did you... Are you off shift?"

"Just finished." He looked older, eyes shadowed and mouth drawn. "I'm hanging in. Ridley found Kinsey's campsite—did he tell you?"

Donna nodded. "I know they found a photo he had of your sister..."

"And the gun he threatened us with on the beach. It's been fired recently."

Pain lanced through her at the hopelessness in his voice. "I'm sorry."

He looked out over the boats. "Still some loose ends. Why come and steal her suitcase from the house? Why did Fran show up at the hospital? How did Kinsey contact Mooch to bust him out?"

And where is his sister's body? Donna's mind pitched in.

Brent sighed. "Thing is, with Kinsey gone, I may never find my sister."

Pain lanced through her at the hopelessness in his voice. "I'm sorry. I just want you to know we… Pacific Coast Investigations, I mean, are still looking into those loose ends."

"Thank you. I appreciate that." He wiped a hand over the brim of his cap.

"No problem." She shrugged. There seemed to be more he wanted to say.

"Do you want to come aboard?" he said hastily. "For some coffee?"

She looked for signs that it was merely a pleasantry, a courtesy like "Let's do lunch" or "I'll call you some-time," but there was sincerity in those haunted eyes. Brent wanted to talk.

"I'd like that."

His broad shoulders seemed to relax a notch as he un-locked the gate and led her over the rain-slicked dock to the boat. The inside was spacious, if worn, and cozy, a welcome respite from the rain. He fired up the coffeepot and poured them both a cup.

Brent gripped the mug. "Kinsey said something to me before he died. He asked me why I would save someone who didn't deserve it. Said his mom told him that's what grace was."

She sighed. "I guess it is. You don't earn it—you just get it."

"I think I've been getting some of that."

"What?"

He sighed. "Grace, even though I don't deserve it."

"Brent, you're a rescue swimmer. You put your life on

the line for strangers all the time. You deserve plenty of grace."

He shifted. "I've been approaching my rescues as a way to get back at God for Carrie, to show Him that I can decide who lives and who dies." She heard the range of emotions, confusion, anger, sorrow, fear.

"But it isn't true. I only get to save them when He lets me."

She stayed quiet and let him speak.

"When Kinsey said that to me, it made me realize that I've been blessed by this job, every day, every save, even every one we didn't save."

"How do you mean?"

"I am privileged to be that guy who drops in from the sky and gives comfort in a moment that nobody else can."

Donna watched the wonder unfold on his face like a bird unfurling its wings to the sky. Still she stayed silent.

"How can I feel blessed?" he suddenly demanded, putting his mug down so hard it sloshed coffee on the table. "My sister is missing and I may never find her. I should be even angrier at God than I was before. Why have I changed?" His gaze swiveled to hers. "Why?"

She smiled and gave him a shrug. "I'm just a veterinarian detective, Brent. How should I know the answer to that?"

He did not smile. "I think it's because I've known you."

She blinked, floored by his words. "I'm no kind of a role model."

"Yes, you are. You're grieving, hurt, scared, angry, but you still turn to God and thank Him for your blessings even when He says no to your prayers."

She felt as though her heart would burst that Brent Mitchell had somehow, someway, been drawn closer to God because of her.

"Two-way street," she managed. "I was having a real

hard time letting Christmas joy in this year until you lent a hand."

He smiled, lifting the shadows from his careworn face for a moment. "Yeah, me and my mad gingerbread skills. I told you I was a genius."

She laughed.

"Anyway," he said, "I know we aren't going to be seeing much of each other anymore, but I wanted to make sure I told you that."

Her joy drifted away. He would return to his life, better for having known her and encountering the grace of God, but his journey would not include Donna. It was the truth she'd known and dreaded, and now she could not ignore it any longer.

"I'm glad for you." She pushed out the words, lips stinging with the effort.

His phone buzzed and he answered. As he listened, something changed on his face. It was as if the light inside him had been extinguished by whatever words he'd just heard.

She put down her cup and braced herself for what she was about to hear.

"Thank you," he said before hanging up.

"Brent, what's wrong?"

His eyes were wild, tormented. He pushed by her, jogging to the deck, where he clasped the wet rail between whitened fingers.

"What is it?"

He breathed hard. "I thought I'd be ready for it."

Dread surged through her body, prickling her skin. She put a palm on his back, feeling his muscles rigid with tension.

"It was Ridley. They found something else at Kinsey's campsite."

She held her breath.

"Pauline's scarf." He swallowed with a gulping sound. "It's got her hair fibers on it…and her blood."

Donna's heart broke for him. He turned and she embraced him, his tears mingling with hers.

TWENTY

Donna could only breathe silent prayers an hour later after Brent lapsed into silence, his raging, the pouring out of memories and fear, subsiding into stillness. She managed to lead him inside and get him to sit down. He slumped on the bench seat. She sat next to him, holding his hand until he dozed. After he'd worked a twenty-four-hour shift and learned about Ridley's grisly find, she could not blame him. At least sleep provided an escape, if only for a moment.

She could not resist passing her fingers over his hair, tracing his profile, memorizing every detail of him, from the tiny scar on his cheekbone to the full curve of his lower lip. Those would be the details she would call up from her memory after Brent had walked out of her life for good. She got up to search for a blanket to cover him when her phone vibrated. She moved away to keep from waking Brent. "Hello?"

There was a high-pitched rapid-fire voice on the other end of the line.

"It's two more weeks until Christmas," she finally made out.

"Harvey? Is that you?"

"Miss Pauline always comes two weeks before the festival to help me pick out my Christmas Eve sweater. It's night and she hasn't come."

"I'm sorry, Harvey. Miss Pauline, um… She isn't back from her trip yet. Would you like me to come over and help you pick out something to wear?"

Brent appeared at her elbow, gesturing for her to let him hear. She put it on speakerphone.

"It's two weeks before," he said. "She always helps me."

She struggled to find the words. "Harvey, there's a chance that Miss Pauline has had some trouble and won't be able to come."

"Trouble?" More silence. "Maybe you should call the number."

"What number?"

"The number from the person who called."

"Called when?"

"The day she left on her trip. I answered the phone for her because she was bathing Radar. She said he'd gotten mixed up with a skunk. Radar can be naughty."

"Harvey," Donna said firmly, "I'm going to come over right now and help you pick out your sweater and you can tell me all about that number, okay?"

There was a long pause. "Can you bring Radar?"

"Yes, of course."

Donna disconnected. Brent was already reaching for his wallet and keys.

"Harvey could be confused," Donna said.

"Right," Brent said. His face blazed with a dangerous mixture of grief and something else. "I'll drive this time."

She didn't argue.

Harvey kept his eyes on Radar, who was thrilled to bask in his undivided attention. Brent knew he was too keyed up to handle the questioning and he was grateful that Donna took charge.

"Harvey, you were holding Pauline's phone when she was bathing Radar and someone called. Do you remember the number?"

Harvey rattled it off. "Miss Pauline told me not to answer, so the caller left a message."

Donna kept her voice soft. "Harvey, do you know what the message was?"

He avoided looking at them, brushing the dog in fast, even strokes.

"We need to know what the caller said. It's important."

Harvey shook his head.

"It was not a nice caller, was it?"

He shook his head.

"Please, Harvey. Tell us what the person said."

Harvey's lips twitched. "He asked if she got the roses and they cost a lot, more than twenty dollars. He said that she was a bad little girl for ignoring him and she should listen to him."

Donna jerked as if she'd been slapped.

Bad little girl. A cold wave swept over Brent and he caught the terror on Donna's face. "Those were his exact words, Harvey?"

Harvey nodded.

Brent went for the door. Donna told Harvey she would be back tomorrow to help him pick out a Christmas sweater. Harvey pleaded with her to let Radar stay and Donna gave in. "Just for a little while, okay, Harvey? Keep him inside with you. I'll call Mr. Carpenter and let him know. I'm sure he'll say yes since it's Miss Pauline's dog."

Donna hopped in as Brent gunned the engine.

"I'll call the police," she said, dialing.

He didn't answer as he fought the urge to stomp on the gas pedal.

"Will Harvey's statement be enough to bring Darius in?"

"No, not unless they can find Pauline's cell phone or Ridley feels there's enough to the story to get a warrant to search Darius's phone records."

"Brent," she said, putting a hand on his arm. "This is a bad idea, going to see him. Darius is crazy."

"He's going to tell me where my sister is," he said through gritted teeth.

"We should let the police handle it."

He pushed the car faster until they arrived at Darius's shop. It was nearly seven, but a light shone in the front office.

"Stay in the car and wait for Ridley." He didn't wait for her answer before he was pushing through the front door.

Darius looked up from the cardboard box he was packing. "Sorry, pal. If you're looking for a whale-watching trip, you'll have to look elsewhere. I'm out of business."

Brent got right up in his face. "You're gonna tell me what you did to my sister."

Donna raced through the door.

"Are we back to that? I told you I didn't know her hardly at all."

Brent slammed a palm on the box. Darius didn't flinch but something flickered to life in his eyes. "You did. You sent her flowers. You called her cell."

Fran raced in. "What is going on?"

Brent hardly noticed. "Your devoted fiancé called my sister and left a threatening message on her phone."

For a split second, fear stoked in Darius's eyes. Then he relaxed. "And I suppose you've got proof of that?"

Brent pressed closer. "That's why you're packing, isn't it? You're going to run because things are starting to spiral out of control. The proof is coming out."

"Packing?" Fran said. "We weren't going to move until next year, Darius. You promised."

"Not now, Frannie," he snapped.

Her mouth clamped shut, her cheeks flushing red.

"You loved Pauline, and she didn't want anything to do with you," Donna said. "That's what happened, isn't it? She hurt your pride, brushed you off."

"So what?" Darius said. "So what if she did? Little stuck-up number like that thinks I'm not good enough for her? Doesn't want to hang out with a guy who smells like sweat and scrubs decks for a living?"

Fran clamped a hand over her mouth.

"Yeah," Brent said, fury rising in his gut. "She'd never go for a guy like you."

"No," Darius spat. "She'd spend every waking moment, every single second, worrying about some strung-out addict. Your sister was a bleeding heart, a stupid little girl. College degree, fancy house, too highbrow for the likes of me."

"I guess I'm just the lowbrow second choice," Fran said. "Is that it?"

"Darius has treated you badly, too, Fran," Brent said. "Running around after other women while he's engaged. What a prize."

Darius glared at Brent. "But now your sister's gone, isn't she? Stupid girl. Stupid, silly little girl is just plain gone and it's eating you up." He laughed.

Brent's vision went fuzzy and he dived for Darius. They tumbled over backward. He was vaguely aware of Ridley slamming through the door, followed by Marco two seconds later.

Marco hauled Brent to his feet and Ridley did the same with Darius.

Fury still boiled in his veins and he nearly ripped himself out of Marco's grasp. "He killed my sister," he shouted.

Marco's arm went around Brent's throat and his struggles were useless against the choke hold.

Darius shook the hair out of his eyes. "This guy is crazy. He came in here after business hours and attacked me. I want him arrested."

Ridley shoved Darius in a chair and another officer stood with him. "You stay put."

Marco marched Brent outside. Ridley and Donna followed and she retold Harvey's revelation about the cell phone message.

Sucking in deep breaths, Brent loosed himself from Marco's grip.

"You're right," Ridley said to Donna, "that's not enough to arrest him, since we don't have the phone, but I'll get started on a search warrant."

"He's packing," Brent snapped. "He's gonna bolt."

"That's the way the system works, Brent," Ridley said.

Brent fought for calm. "We're two miles from the Mexican border here. He'll vanish if you don't take him in now."

"I told you, I can't do that."

"If you can't stop him, I will." Brent evaded Marco's restraining arm, but Ridley stepped in his way.

"Listen to me," he grunted. "I'm trying not to arrest you here, because I know what that's going to do to your career."

Brent breathed hard through his nose. "He's guilty."

"Maybe, but don't ruin yourself trying to prove that."

Brent stared at Ridley. "I thought you'd be happy to see me drummed out of the coast guard."

"I thought I would be, too." Ridley scrubbed a hand over his face. "I guess things change. I still despise you, mind you, but I don't want to see you stripped of everything. It's tough enough to lose your sister. I can have a search warrant first thing in the morning."

"That's too long."

"Best I can do. Even if we can prove he called and threatened her, it doesn't put him on the beach that day or in any way link him to Bruce's accident. I just got a text that San Diego PD arrested Mooch. We'll see where that gets us." He gripped Brent's shoulder. "Stay away from Darius."

Ridley went inside.

Brent braced his arms on the wood railing, fighting for control. He felt Donna's approach.

"Brent…" she said.

He shook his head. "Ridley's right. We shouldn't be here. Go home, Donna."

"I'll drive you back to the boat."

He turned to her then, wanting more than anything to put his face against hers and press the world away. "No."

"You're not staying here."

He didn't answer.

"Brent," she said. "If you try to get in there and search yourself, you'll be arrested. It will end your career."

He took a breath. "I know what the stakes are."

"Darius will kill you." She put her hands around his neck and her fingers sent tingles along his spine. "Please come away from here. Please."

If it were any other question, he would have been powerless to say no to her.

"Marco will make sure you get home safely," he said, his voice breaking midsentence.

Marco nodded.

"Please," she whispered, tears filling her eyes. "Please don't do this. Your sister wouldn't want you to risk your life."

He could only look at her, amazed that she cared enough to cry for him, overwhelmed with the blessing of it all.

She clung to him and for a moment, he clutched her close, feeling the rapid beat of her heart, breathing in the sweet scent of her hair.

"You need to go home, Donna."

"What can I do to help you?" she whispered.

"Pray for me. That's enough." Then he kissed the top of her head and pulled her away, Marco helping.

Marco put an arm around her shoulders and turned her toward the car, giving Brent one last look.

"Are you going to tell me I'm crazy?" Brent asked him.

Marco shrugged. "You are, Coastie, but in my experience, sometimes a little crazy is necessary to get the job done."

"Marco, what did you say your assignment was in the navy, anyway?"

"I didn't." He nodded. "Don't get killed."

"Yes, sir."

Donna let Marco drive her back to retrieve Radar and then took them home.

"Lock the door." He put a gentle hand on her forearm. "Done all you can for Coastie. He's gonna be okay."

"How do you know that?"

"Just do," he said. "He's tough—he'll get through."

He stood on the porch until she locked the door behind her. The night faded into silence. She fed Radar and prowled around the house, pacing futile circles on the hardwood until she found herself at the foot of her pathetic Christmas tree. She saw her own reflection in the single gold ball that Brent had placed there.

It's more hopeful somehow.

Her life was more hopeful since Brent had been delivered into it. He brought back the joy, the laughter, her desire to become involved with other people's lives. Because of Brent, she realized, she'd learned to trust herself again. She put a fingertip to the shiny surface. If Brent was going to risk everything to find his sister, she was not going to let him do it alone. She could not ask him to build a life with her, but she could be his partner until the case was closed, however it turned out.

Grabbing her keys, she headed back out into the night.

TWENTY-ONE

Brent waited under the shelter of a tree for what seemed like days, though it was only three hours. It was nearing midnight when Darius finally drove out of the marina parking lot, Fran beside him in the passenger seat. He could not see her well in the gloom, but her head was down, profile dejected.

Run while you can, he wanted to tell her. *While you're still alive.* As soon as they cleared the parking lot, he sauntered down the paved walkway, past the docks and the restaurants locked up tight. He was grateful that Darius's shop was at the far end of the marina, away from any suspicious eyes. They had security, no doubt, so he kept to the shadows as best he could. He made it to the back door without anybody stopping him. It was locked, but he noticed a window slightly ajar.

His pulse pounded. Breaking and entering was a crime. He would lose his career. But what if this was his only chance, the one moment he would have to find out what had happened to his sister? Could he risk the most important thing in his life?

The reality of it came home to him at that moment. The most important thing in his life was the people he'd been given to love. Period. Reaching for the window, he slid it open and hoisted himself up over the sill.

Dropping down onto the hallway floor, he crouched there for a moment listening before making his way along. The hallway opened up onto a small room with an unmade bed and piles of magazines everywhere. Beauty magazines that someone, probably Fran, had dog-eared and rifled through until their covers were tattered. An old TV and a fishing rod in the corner were the only other embellishments. He continued down the hallway. The next door was closed, latched and locked by a padlock. Brent's pulse revved up. If there was any evidence to help him find his sister, it would be in here. He hurried to the bathroom and found a tweezer and a safety pin and bent them both at the tip. Inserting the tweezer as a tension rod, he raked the safety pin in the keyhole. He was grateful his coastie buddies liked to play pranks. Burglarizing each other's lockers was a regular pastime. In moments, the lock popped open.

He pushed in. The room was cold. He dared not turn on the light, instead using a penlight on his key chain to see. The contents of the room were boxed and labeled. Darius really was intending to leave soon. There was one box separate from the others and not yet taped shut. He reached for it and shone the light inside.

A photo of his sister's face shone back at him, nearly startling him into dropping the flashlight. It was not one photo but many, obviously taken with a zoom lens when she was unaware. Pauline at work laughing with Harvey, unlocking her own front door, jogging near the marina. The last one made him stop short. Pauline on the remote beach where he feared she'd been killed, her rainbow scarf fluttering in the breeze, hair blown across her face.

It was a snapshot of his sister on the last day of her life.

"Figured you'd come back," Darius said, shoving the stun gun against Brent's neck and pressing the button.

Donna saw no sign of Brent until she caught sight of the open window and guessed he might be inside. She prayed he would find something that would put an end to the agonizing limbo and get out quickly.

She waited in the shadows of the bushes. One minute stretched to two, then five, and still there was no sign of him. A taxi pulled up in the marina and Fran got out, hugging herself as she walked along the path. She tried the back door and found it locked. She whacked her palm against the door until it opened.

"What are you making that racket for?" Darius growled. "I told you how things were. I got nothing more to say."

"You're not going to dump me like some bag of trash," she said. "I've been with you since we were sixteen. We were going to get married." Her voice took on a pleading note. "I love you."

"Look, Frannie, you're a good girl and it's been great, but I'm leaving and I'm not coming back. You aren't gonna be happy in Mexico, so it's best we call it quits."

Her back stiffened, arms straight at her sides. "You can't leave me," she rasped. "I know you used Kinsey's car to kill Bruce Gallagher."

Donna froze.

Darius took a step toward Fran and she flinched back. "You aren't going to tell the cops, Frannie, because then you'll be in trouble for staying quiet about it."

"There's something else I know..." She spoke so softly Donna almost didn't catch it.

"You don't know anything." Darius's face was monstrous in the meager light.

"What if I knew the truth about what you did to Pauline?"

"You won't tell," he said. "If you're smart."

She sucked in a breath, fighting tears. "Maybe I will."

He raised a hand, his tone changing. "Aww, Frannie. You've been good to me when no one else was. Pauline didn't mean anything to me."

His voice hitched when he said Pauline's name. Donna wondered if Fran heard it, also.

"I'll get set up in Mexico, find us a place. Then I'll send for you. Okay?"

"Okay," she said.

Darius smiled. "That's a good girl. I've gotta get packed up now before that cop comes back."

Fran allowed him to press a kiss on her cheek before he closed the door again. She stood staring, motionless, until finally she hustled back to the waiting cab.

Darius might think he'd persuaded Fran, but the ferocity Donna glimpsed on her face as she passed by told the true story. Fran knew that he'd loved Pauline. And she also knew, or suspected, that he'd killed her.

Donna hoped Fran was on her way to the police station to tell everything she knew about Darius Fields. At the moment, she was more concerned with another matter. What had happened to Brent?

Brent still felt the agony of the electrical charge roaring through his body. When his senses returned, he found himself lying on his back on the floor, his hands secured with a plastic zip tie. Darius entered the room, smiling down at him.

"Think you're so special with your coast guard credentials and your fancy boat. Not feeling so fancy now, are you?"

Brent tried to focus his blurry vision. "What did you do to my sister?"

"I killed her, stupid."

Those words bored into his soul, nearly driving the breath from his body. "Why? What did she ever do to you?"

"She brushed me off, treated me like a nobody."

"She didn't. I know my sister. She never treated anyone like that in her whole life."

Darius wasn't listening. "So high and mighty. Too good to give me the time of day for anything but my little boat tours. Then I come to find out she hired Bruce Gallagher to investigate me for beating up Kinsey and torching his trailer. Little worm had it coming because he stole from me. Did she ever consider that? That I was the victim, not Kinsey? No, and the worm sees me on the beach with Pauline." He grimaced, eyes rolling. "I just wanted to talk to her, to ask her to call off Gallagher, but she wouldn't listen. Things got out of hand and Kinsey saw the whole thing."

"So you killed him, too?"

"Had to sell my boat to pay off Mooch and his people. My boat," Darius roared. "I got nothing now, thanks to Kinsey. Mooch was happy to take a little side job and get Kinsey out of the hospital so I could tow him out to sea and leave him to drown. Better than Kinsey deserved."

Brent struggled to get to his feet, but Darius delivered a hard kick to the side of his head, sending him back to the floor.

"You're not smart enough to get away," Brent panted, blood trickling down his face.

"Oh, yeah? Maybe I will get caught on my way to the border," Darius said with a laugh, "but you'll already be dead by then, so you won't be around to gloat. Let's go, coast guard hero."

Maybe I was wrong, Donna thought to herself. Maybe Brent had thought better of the idea and hadn't gone into Darius's office. Or it could be he'd been and gone. Donna was reaching in her jacket pocket for her phone when Darius came out again, hauling something behind him. In a moment of sick horror, she realized it was Brent, his hands tied, stumbling.

"Come on." Darius shoved Brent. Brent stopped, aiming a kick at Darius that never reached its target. There was a crackle of electricity, a sizzle of light and Brent dropped to the ground, twitching.

Donna wanted to run to him. Instead, she clapped a hand over her mouth to contain the scream. Darius picked

Brent up, tossed him over his shoulder and walked toward the parking lot.

Her mind whirled. She had to call the police, but she didn't dare take her eyes off Darius and Brent. If they got out of her sight, he might be dead before the police arrived. Keeping to the shadows, she hurried after them so quickly that she skidded on a rock. The noise sounded loud in the darkness and Darius stopped.

Donna dived behind a trash can and waited, her heart thundering. When she dared to peek around the edge of the can, Darius was walking fast, nearly jogging to the parking lot. She stayed as close as she dared and saw him dump Brent in the back of his truck and head out of the lot, towing a small motorboat on a rig behind him.

Giving him a head start, she drove after him, praying she would not lose him. Hands numb with icy terror, she found her phone and pressed a button.

"Marco," she pleaded, "please pick up."

He answered on the second ring. "Where are you?"

"Following Darius. He's heading for the bridge. Brent is unconscious and he's taking him somewhere." She told him what she'd overheard Fran say.

"Pull over. Stop following," he barked. "Right now."

"I can't, Marco. Darius is going to kill him."

"Donna, I mean it. Pull over right now."

"I'm sorry, Marco," she said.

Brent drifted in and out of consciousness, finally coming to at the feel of the waves slapping against the side of the motorboat.

Darius piloted the craft away from shore as Brent tried to get his bearings.

"The police know everything," Brent said. "You're wasting effort killing me."

"Oh, I don't think it's a wasted effort," Darius called

over the motor. "I'm going to enjoy killing you. And drowning." He laughed. "Don't you think that's the perfect irony, to drown a coast guard hero? There are no boaters out where I'm taking you. No one to call in for help."

Brent tried to figure out where exactly they were. He saw enough of the coastline to realize that Darius was going to dump him in the ocean near the caves at the foot of Coronado Bluff. It was a good choice, he thought ruefully, because the storm-tossed waves were going to drive him immediately into those caves and batter him to pieces on the rocks. He'd be dead within minutes.

Except that Brent had other plans.

When Darius slowed the boat, he kicked hard and took the legs out from underneath him. Darius went down only partially, grabbing again for his stun gun. One more shock and Brent would be out and powerless, so he took the only choice he had. He leaped overboard.

Darius tried to grab him, his eyes burning with fury. Then a smile wreathed his face. "Okay, hero. If that's the way you want to play it, so be it. Don't take too long to drown." He yanked the boat around and raced away over the waves.

Brent felt the cold seep through his body. With his hands bound, he had to rely on his legs to keep him above the waterline. The shore was a half mile away, which would have been attainable if he could use his arms. Tugging against the binding, he realized there was no way he could loosen the plastic ties. He put his head down and kicked with all his might, but the waves continued to tow him, in spite of his efforts, toward the mouth of the cave. The current gained power.

He paused, gasping for breath, his body still aching from the stun gun attack.

Come on, Brent. Time for you to save yourself.

* * *

Donna screeched the truck to a halt at the top of the bluff, which looked down over the ocean. She saw Darius zooming away in the boat, but there was no sign of Brent.

Where are you?

Her body was taut with fear as she grabbed the tiny binoculars from her glove box. With only moonlight for help, she could see nothing.

Where? Could she have been wrong? Was Brent still in Darius's boat? Should she follow as best she could from the road? Paralyzed with indecision, she peered once more through the binoculars. A tiny glimmer of color, the white of a face, shone against the gray waves.

Brent.

He was being carried toward the mouth of the cave. Even if Marco got the coast guard to deploy immediately, it would be too late for Brent. She fired a quick text to tell Marco of her location.

Frantically, she scanned her car for anything floatable. She saw Tracy's life vest, left in her car from their last visit to the beach. It was child sized, but it was the only thing she had. Quickly, she dialed 911 on her phone. When the dispatcher answered, she yelled, "There's a man drowning outside the caves at Coronado Bluff. I'm going in after him."

"Ma'am," the dispatcher said, "please do not…"

The words faded away as she tucked the life vest over her arm and crashed into the surf.

TWENTY-TWO

Brent knew he was on his way toward losing consciousness. His shivering had slowed and he was starting to feel drowsy. *Come on, Brent, rescue swimmer training was harder than this.*

He flipped on his back to rest for a minute, and the water continued to shove him toward the cave. The roar of the waves crashing inside reminded him what would happen to an incapacitated swimmer. He'd be tossed against those rock walls and it would be lights out.

Once more, he turned over and started kicking with all his strength. His brain told him it was fruitless effort; without his arms he was at the whim of the ocean. Because his brain wasn't going to answer for his body, he pushed on, fighting through the numbing cold and sting of water. Inexorably, he was sucked toward the mouth of the cave.

Praying for a new reserve of strength, he kicked harder, his body sinking lower and lower until he began to swallow mouthfuls of salt water. Coughing, eyes stinging, he felt his reserves drain away. All around was nothing but an uncrossable expanse of ocean.

This was what it felt like, he realized, to those victims he'd plucked out of the water when all their hope of rescue had faded. What he wouldn't have given to see an orange coast guard helicopter at that moment, a rescue swimmer rappelling down a cable. Oddly, he felt a surge of happiness knowing that he had been that comfort, that miracle, for dozens of victims. Not through his power and skill, but because God had allowed him to be there when he was needed the most. The honor of it tingled inside him, the privilege of being blessed by God to bless others.

He had not been granted the ability to help Carrie, but finally, as the water pushed him slowly under, he came to peace with it.

Another wall of water doused him, holding him under until his lungs burned. The cold was painful now, and he imagined he heard voices. A hand grabbed the back of his shirt and pulled him upright.

He gaped in shock as Donna stared back at him.

He blinked, wondering if he was hallucinating as she shoved a tiny life vest around his neck.

"How…?"

"I followed Darius. Help is coming."

"Donna," he said, spitting out a mouthful of water. "You've got to swim back." He held up his hands. "I can't get us to shore with my wrists tied."

"I know," she said. Her mane of hair was plastered around her. "I'm not strong enough, either, but we're going to stay afloat until the coast guard arrives, I can promise you that."

"No," he started again, desperate to see her back to safety. "Go back to shore."

"Listen, Brent," she said, grabbing the edge of his life vest. "You're not the rescuer here at this moment, so get used to it. We're gonna do this together."

He wanted to shove her toward the beach, to propel her back to safety against her stubborn protests, but he couldn't. The cave was so close now he could feel the vibrations of the surf crashing against the rock. "Please," he said. "You've got to get out of here."

She shoved her sodden hair from her face. "I thought I told you that Gallagher women are stubborn stock."

"Donna…"

She held two cold fingers to his lips. "Partners stick together until the case is closed."

He shut his eyes. How long could they stay afloat? Would

he witness her being sucked away, broken and battered against the rock walls? Another woman he loved taken by the ocean, and him helpless to do anything about it. He forced himself higher in the water. "We have to keep from being swept into that cave."

He could tell she was tired, cold, her shoulders lower in the water. He gestured for her to turn her back to him, and then he looped his bound arms over her shoulders. "I can kick for us."

She nodded, cleaving the waves with her hands as he propelled with his feet. They made several yards of progress until her strokes became weak and they were gradually sucked back again.

"Where is that chopper?" she moaned. "I thought you guys were fast."

"They'll be here. A few more minutes." But nothing appeared as he scanned the predawn sky. It would take them time to deploy and to locate two swimmers in these choppy waters. It was time they didn't have.

"Donna," he said one more time. "I want you to go. You can still make it if you aren't dragging me."

She turned in his arms then, wrapping him in a ferocious embrace. "We're going to ride this out together because we're partners, Brent Mitchell." She pressed her cold mouth to his and kissed him. "Now keep kicking."

With the feel of that kiss, strong and tender at the same time, he kicked on.

The minutes ticked by in slow motion. Donna tried to hang on to Brent, but her arms were so cold they went numb. Her finger muscles had deadened into useless lumps. The life preserver was suddenly ripped away from Brent's neck.

"Hold on to me," she yelled.

He could not answer as he whirled out of her grasp.

"Brent!" she screamed, and then there was a splashing nearby and Marco appeared, holding Brent by the shirt.

"I am so glad to see you," Donna panted.

"All the ladies say that," Marco said. He pulled a knife from his belt and sliced the zip ties from Brent's wrists. "Can you make it now, Coastie?"

Exhausted as he was, Brent managed a nod.

"Put this on." He thrust a life jacket into Donna's hands. "Hold on to me. We're gonna swim toward shore. I would have brought a boat but I didn't have time to find one."

They'd gotten only a few yards, with Marco shouting commands at Brent, who was barely managing a crawl, when the coast guard cutter *Haddock* drew near, searchlights probing the water, orange stripe standing out boldly in the gloom. Donna had never realized how utterly beautiful a ship could be.

She held on to Brent, while Marco waved his hands and signaled the boat. A smaller boat launched from the cutter and within moments they'd been brought aboard the quicker vessel, blankets thrown around them, a coast guard sailor checking them over, trying to extract information from Brent.

"ETA to the dock is five minutes," the sailor said. "Ambulance is waiting." He shot a glance at Brent. "Man, if we'd known it was you, we'd have sent the helicopter so you could hitch a ride on your own bird."

Brent managed a wave. "Believe me, the small boat is just fine."

He was weak and freezing cold, but hearing the strength returning to his voice relieved the massive weight from Donna's shoulders.

A look of surprise crossed the sailor's face as he listened to his radio. "Just got a message from an Officer Ridley. He's reporting that your man Darius Fields has been apprehended and is on his way to jail."

Brent heaved out a breath. "Then that makes this whole midnight swim worth it."

"What about Fran?" Donna asked through chattering teeth.

"They'll question her but unless they can prove she knew about the murder, there's not a whole lot they can do," Marco said.

Donna chafed Brent's frigid hands as they motored to the dock. She could see the beautiful San Diego skyline. Some of the skyscrapers were outlined in red-and-green Christmas lights. She saw their sparkle reflected in Brent's eyes, but the light did not seem to penetrate.

Heavenly Father, she wanted to say aloud, to thank Him for delivering them from the ocean, but the anguish on Brent's face took her breath away. They were alive, but now he had to come to grips once and for all with the fact that Darius had indeed murdered his sister. She settled on a silent prayer of thanksgiving and a plea that God would ease the pain that coursed through him.

The ambulance was waiting as promised. Brent insisted on climbing in under his own power. Marco refused to go at all, but he helped Donna get in.

Brent reached out a hand and shook Marco's solemnly. "Thanks, man."

Marco nodded.

"You handle yourself well in rough seas. What did you say you did for the navy?"

This time, Marco allowed a small grin. "I didn't. Meet you at the hospital," he said before the doors closed.

Brent let the medics strap a blood pressure cuff on and she did the same.

They rode in silence until Brent finally spoke. "I always thought I was the rescuer, the guy who pulled others out of the mess, and today two people had to pull me out."

"I didn't pull you out. If Marco hadn't arrived just then, I don't think we would have made it."

He raised an eyebrow. "Still, you came in after me, and I got to see a hero through the victim's eyes."

She flushed. "I'm not a hero."

He pressed his lips to her hand. "Donna, I've seen plenty of people act bravely in my time in the coast guard, but I've never seen anyone do what you did for me tonight."

She thought she detected a flush of pink on his pale cheeks. "Does it…make you feel uncomfortable?"

"A little bit," he admitted, "but I'll get over it. I guess I was about due for some humbling. I just wish I could have been there, or anyone could have been there, to help Pauline when she needed it."

Donna squeezed his hand. "I'm sorry."

"Me, too, because I know I'm never going to get over it." His voice dropped to a whisper. "I did not save my sister."

She pulled the blanket tighter around his shoulders, the only way she could think of to comfort him now.

It was nearing two o'clock in the morning when the doctors finished their poking and prodding. Donna gratefully slipped into the dry clothes her sisters had brought and tiptoed to Sarah's hospital room, summoned by her younger sister. Her mother was there, and Candace and Angela, and they wasted no time wrapping her in a tight embrace.

"Not cool," Candace said. "You promised to stay safe."

Donna was about to answer when Brent limped into her room, wearing clothes that Marco had driven over to get for him.

"I just wanted to say goodbye," he said. His face was bruised; a five-o'clock shadow darkened his chin.

"You shouldn't be up and about," Donna said. "The doctors want you to stay."

He accepted gentle hugs from Candace, Angela and JeanBeth. "I hate hospitals."

"You and me both," Sarah muttered.

JeanBeth hugged him and so did the sisters, mumbling sympathies and condolences. Brent shifted uncomfortably under the attention.

"Anyway, I figured I'd pop in on my way out."

"I can't stay too long, either," Angela said. "I've got Radar in the car. I picked him up from Open Vistas like you asked me to earlier, but he doesn't seem to like my cat. Harvey didn't want to give him back, but the Open Vista's manager was happy to see him go. I think he chewed up a TV remote."

"I still haven't figured out what to do with Radar," Brent said sadly.

"I'll take him," Donna said. "He's happy at my place."

"And here's the address for Fran's rental property." Angela handed her a piece of paper.

Donna stared at it, thinking about Fran's encounter with Darius.

"Are you listening to me?" Angela prodded.

"Yes. I was just thinking about something Fran said to Darius. I thought she was his victim all along, but she knew he'd killed Dad and she covered for him. I'm sure of it, even if the police can't prove that."

Candace shook her head. "How could she do that? Did she love him that much that she'd cover up murder?"

"And that suitcase," Donna mused. "I can't get it out of my mind. Why would Kinsey bother stealing a suitcase with Pauline's things? He only wanted the money."

Brent stood up straight, wincing as the action pulled on his ribs. "Police interviewed her but didn't make an arrest. I'm going to check out her rental place right now. I'm too banged up to manage my motorcycle. Can I borrow your car one more time, Donna?"

"Only if I'm in it."

Brent and Marco shook their heads in unison.

"Oh, no," Marco said. "Our ocean adventure was plenty for one day."

"This trip is on dry ground."

"You can find trouble anywhere, dry ground or not," Marco said firmly.

"Look," she said. "If we're going to run Dad's investigation firm, we have to be thorough and not afraid to take risks…like Dad was."

"Are we? Running Dad's firm, I mean?" Candace folded her arms across her chest. "Dad's murder is solved. Are we really going to keep the investigation business going considering we're not private eyes in any way, shape or form?"

Donna sucked in a breath. "I guess that depends on you three."

"Oh, I'm in," Sarah said from the bed. "I'm done being the victim. I'm ready to take down bad guys and serve up some justice for once."

Angela laughed. "Well, I can see I'm going to need to stick around and keep the peace." Her voice faltered. "Since I'll be stateside for a while."

"I guess I can file things at least and answer phones." Candace sighed. "Marco, can you stand to have four Gallagher women mucking up the works?"

"Five," their mother said, clearing her throat. "Your father would be proud of you girls. I'm certain of that."

Marco threw up his hands. "This is insane."

"That's his way of saying, 'What a stupendous idea,'" Candace said with a chuckle.

"So how do we proceed?" Angela asked.

"Brent and I are going to check out Fran's rental place. It's probably nothing, but maybe we can dig up something that might help the cops prove she knew about Pauline's murder." She held up a hand. "No more breaking and entering, right, Brent?"

"Yes, ma'am."

Marco started to speak, but Donna interrupted.

"And Marco will follow along like our big scary shadow, right?"

"I'm missing out on everything," Sarah complained.

"I'll stay here with you." Angela said. "They've promised to release you today and there's some talk of awarding you the 'worst-behaved patient' award."

"Let me see if I can push things along downstairs," JeanBeth said. "I know a nurse on the night shift."

Donna and Brent headed to the car and retrieved Radar from Angela's vehicle. The dog greeted them with a thorough licking. Donna slid into the passenger's seat and tossed Brent the keys.

He raised an eyebrow. "You're volunteering to let me drive?"

"Sure."

He frowned. "You don't need to treat me with kid gloves. I know my sister is gone, Donna. Nothing we learn about Fran will bring her back." He started the engine. "But maybe it will help us serve up a little justice. Besides, like you said, we're in it until the case is closed."

Closed and she and Brent returned to their own lives.

"Right," she said brightly. "Let's get it over with, then."

She thought he hesitated for a moment before he started the car, but she kept her eyes trained out the front window, careful not to look at the face of the man she would have to learn how to lose.

TWENTY-THREE

Brent parked across the street from Fran's house in Imperial Beach. It was nearly dawn. The structure was not in pristine condition, an older ranch-style home in need of more white paint, with black shutters framing the windows. The lawn was dead, nothing more than a scalp of dry grass. Curtains shielded the windows. Fran's car was parked in the driveway. Yellowed newspapers, never read, dotted the porch.

Marco called. "Going to pull around the back, check things out. What are we hoping to find here, Coastie?"

"I don't know. Maybe nothing."

"Copy that." Marco clicked off and pulled around the block, which led to an alley.

"Doesn't look like she's spent much time on the place," Donna said. "She had plans to sell in the future and move to Mexico with Darius."

"Guess his plans were different than hers."

Brent got out. "I'm going to go talk to her."

"What will you say?"

"I want to know how well she knew my sister. Maybe... maybe there's something she will let slip that might indicate she knew what Darius did to her. Or where her body is. At this point, I just need to finish it. Good or bad. I have to know."

"Brent..."

He shook his head. "Don't worry. I know this is probably the last dead end. I'm under control. I promise."

"I'm coming with you." Donna got out and rolled the window down for Radar. "Stay here, boy. Be back soon."

Fran answered on the second knock. A packed suitcase

stood by the door in the dim interior. "What do you want?" she said, eyebrows drawn.

"To ask you a few questions," Brent said.

"Cops already did that. I'm sick of questions."

Radar shoved his head out the car window and barked.

"Are you leaving?" Donna said, pointing to the bag.

"That's none of your business, is it? Darius is in jail. You got what you wanted. Now go away."

"I know how you feel, but you're better off without him," Donna said. "I speak from experience."

Brent watched Fran's face light up with anger. "I'm so sick of people telling me that. My parents, my sister— everyone has always hated Darius."

He was incredulous. "The man's a killer, Fran. Wake up. Sometimes when everyone who loves you is telling you the same thing, it's because they're right."

Fran gripped the door. "Go away."

Radar's barking grew louder.

"Were you covering up my sister's murder, too?" Brent said. "Along with Bruce Gallagher's?"

Her expression wavered. "I'm sorry for what happened to Bruce. I didn't know for sure Darius did it. I only suspected. I would have stopped him if I had known what he was planning."

Brent raised a skeptical eyebrow.

"And I don't know anything about your sister other than she probably got what was coming to her." Her tone hardened. "Teasing Darius, making nice to him so he got his head turned."

"That's not the kind of person my sister is."

"Of course not. She's a good girl, a smart girl, right?"

"You know what?" Brent said slowly. "You sound just like Darius."

Her eyes narrowed and she started to close the door. With an earsplitting bark, Radar leaped through the open car window and bolted up the walk. Fran had not quite gotten the door fully closed when Radar slammed through, shoving Fran back. The dog's barks were deafening.

"Radar, come here," Brent shouted.

The dog beelined to a closed door, barking and clawing at the wood.

"Get him out of here," Fran shouted, "or I'll kill him."

Brent pushed past her.

"You can't come in here. You have no right," she yelled.

Ignoring her, Brent tried the door handle. It was locked, but the lock was cheap. Radar continued to claw and whine at the door.

"Open it," Brent said.

"Get out," Fran rasped. "You can't come into my house and tell me what to do."

Brent heard a muffled cry from the other side of the door. He pounded a fist on the wood. "Open it right now or I'm breaking it down."

Fran didn't move, so Brent launched a kick that splintered the wood. It took two more until he was through. The dog squeezed in first, barking and whining. Brent broke away the splintered wood and crammed himself into the gap. He slammed on the light switch and jogged down the steps, heart in his throat, Donna right behind him.

The breath was sucked from his lungs when he reached the landing.

"Have it your way, then," Fran said, taking a gun from her pocket. "Now you can die with your sister."

Donna's mind reeled. The young woman with a duct-taped mouth, chained to a support beam in the basement, could only be Pauline Mitchell. Brent dropped to his knees.

"Pauline," he rasped.

"Oh, yes, it's sweet Pauline," Fran said.

"I thought…" Donna stammered.

"That Darius killed her?" Fran snorted. "So did he. He left her there, the fool, but who was following along behind? Poor little Frannie. I saw Jeff try to help her. He took her scarf, poor sap. After he left, Pauline came to, and I knew she would go straight to the cops and Darius would go to jail. So who covered up for him? Huh? Who? Who called Open Vistas and left a fake message? Me, and Darius didn't even know it. All this time he's been weeping for her. I was the one who tried to steal her suitcase and plant the note in the house and make it look like she'd gone on a trip. All for Darius. All for him." Bright angry tears shone on Fran's lashes.

Radar whined, licking pitifully at Pauline's cheeks. The woman's eyes were round with fear as she yanked against the chain.

Brent reached to pull the tape from his sister's mouth, but Fran jerked the gun. "Don't do that. I can't stand to hear her yapping. I would have killed her weeks ago but it's harder to hide a body than you'd think. I'll just have to dump her on the beach somewhere, or leave her here in the basement until I get away."

"You can't kill us all," Brent said, straightening, moving closer. He was trying to get himself between Fran's gun and the two women. Donna's heart thwacked against her ribs. She scanned frantically for something to use to help.

"So you're going to let Darius ruin the rest of your life, huh?" Donna said.

Fran flinched. "I gave him everything. I've stood by him since he was sixteen even though it cost me my family. We were going to get married. Have children."

"No, you weren't," Donna said.

"Keep your mouth shut," Fran hissed, her eyes burning. Understanding dawned on Brent's face. He eased closer to Fran as her attention was riveted on Donna.

Fran rubbed a sleeve across her nose. "You don't know anything about me and Darius."

"Oh, yes, I do," Donna said. "Darius used you, strung you along. 'We'll get married someday. We'll have kids someday,' yet he was in love with Pauline and I'm sure she wasn't the first. It was all just lies he told you."

"It was an infatuation with Pauline and the others. What we had was love." Fran gulped.

"Love doesn't include murder. Love doesn't involve running away from your partner to Mexico. Do you really think he was going to send for you?"

"Stop talking," Fran said, her hand shaking on the gun. "I know him. I love him. He's—"

Brent dived before she finished the sentence, crashing into her legs, toppling her over. The gun fired before he knocked it from her hand, and it skidded across the cement floor. Donna screamed as the bullet struck the wooden shelves behind her. She ran toward Pauline to shield her. Radar went wild with barking, running to Brent and entangling Brent's legs in the process. He stumbled and Fran got to her feet and ran for the steps.

Brent finally succeeded in freeing himself from the dog and lurched toward the steps, breathing hard.

Marco appeared at the head of the stairs, holding Fran securely by the wrist. "Coastie?"

"All okay here," Brent panted, scrambling to his sister and enfolding her in a crushing embrace.

Marco nodded. Pauline was crying now, tears flowing down her face as Donna watched Brent gently peel the tape away from her mouth.

"Looks like the case is finally closed," Marco said with a smile.

"Yes, sir," Brent said, his eyes never leaving his sister's face as he stroked her hair.

Marco grinned. "Not bad for a puddle jumper."

Brent clutched his sister, holding her in his arms, chains and all. He looked over her shoulder and reached for Donna's hand. He squeezed her fingers and in the gesture was a world of emotion.

Gratitude, joy, relief and, she imagined, a goodbye.

Case closed, just as Marco had said.

She clutched his fingers for one more moment, and then she let him go.

On Christmas Eve, Donna forced herself to put on her most cheerful sweater, the one festooned with candy canes, and fixed her hair in a loose twist before she delivered her gift to Candace's house. "I wish you'd come with us to the Del instead of going on your own," Candace said.

Donna offered a smile. "I'll meet up with you after a while, I promise. I just need a little time to myself first."

"Okay, hot cocoa and fireworks. Don't be late." She squeezed Donna's fingers. "It's a Gallagher family tradition. I tried to tell Sarah that, but she won't come."

Donna sighed. "She can't. Not right now. Maybe when she's had more time to adjust to being home."

Candace nodded, and Donna saw the shadows under her eyes. "I guess the Gallagher family traditions are going to have to change."

"Only some of them." She clung to her sister and they held each other through the moment of grief. Their first Christmas without their father. Her only comfort was in knowing that Brent was not alone. After Pauline was treated at the hospital for dehydration and a fractured wrist, she had insisted on returning home, with Brent keeping careful watch over her recovery.

Donna had stayed away from their reunion and Brent had contacted her only briefly. He had returned to his duties, joyful that his world was made right again. Donna could not shake the feeling that hers would never be quite right again, without Brent, without her father. Still, in spite of the heartache, she felt at peace, confident in herself for the first time since Nate.

After a final kiss for Candace, she headed to the office. With trembling hands, she placed the finished wooden cable car on the tree and said a prayer for her father. "Love you, Dad. I will miss you every day of my life."

When her tears subsided enough, she headed for the Del. The grand old hotel was awash in glittering lights spangling its red Victorian roof. Outside past the patio, Pauline was watching the ice rink, supervising her charges. She was thin and moved as if she was sore, but the smile on her face was radiant. Harvey's arm was crooked through hers, his other hand holding Radar's leash. Beyond the ice, the ocean glittered in the moonlight.

"I'm watching the ice-skating," Harvey proclaimed to Donna when he saw her.

"Yes, you are," Donna said. "And I'm so glad."

Pauline hugged Donna. "I understand from my boss that you were prepared to step in for me and escort my Open Vistas family to the Del for the festival."

Donna blushed. "I'm so happy it didn't turn out that way."

"You and me both. I don't think I'll ever be able to go to the beach by myself again, even with Radar." She shuddered.

"Are you cold, Miss Pauline?" Harvey asked. "Do you want to wear my sweater?"

Pauline hugged him around the shoulders. "No, thank you, sweetie. I'm warm just being here with you for the festival."

Harvey nodded and returned his gaze to the progress of the skaters clacking along accompanied by strains of Christmas music.

"My brother couldn't have picked a better partner than you."

Donna started. "Oh, we managed to solve the case in spite of ourselves. Is he…working tonight?"

"Oh, you never know with Brent. Even when he is at work, he texts me until I'm ready to scream. That man needs another focus in his life for sure." There was a mischievous sparkle in her eye. "Come on, Harvey. Let's get the gang together and find some cocoa before the fireworks."

Donna watched them go. Beyond the ice-skating rink, the sea crawled back and forth as if it, too, danced to the carols. People laughed and chatted around her, kids drifted in and out of the lobby to see the magnificent tree, and every corner of the historic Hotel Del Coronado was steeped in Christmas cheer. She closed her eyes and tried to lose herself in the music and the scent of hot chocolate.

She opened them when someone jostled her elbow.

Brent stood there, wearing a garish vest and red-and-green scarf.

Her heart jumped to her throat. "I didn't expect to see you."

"Just got off duty," he said with a smile so infectious it made her weak in the knees.

"Nice holiday outfit."

He laughed. "It makes Pauline happy to see me wearing it, even though I get a ribbing from my crew."

"I can't imagine why."

He straightened. "I wanted to give you a Christmas gift."

"No need for that. You already gave me a poinsettia."

He grinned. "Killed it yet?"

She hung her head. "Almost."

He laughed and looked around. "Nothing like Christmas at the Del, is there?"

"Nothing." Her throat thickened as she watched a little girl whizzing around the ice holding her father's hand.

"Thinking about your dad?" he said softly.

She nodded and he reached out to stroke her hair.

"I'm sorry."

"Me, too. But you've got your sister," she said. "And that's a miracle."

"Yes, it is." He sighed. "I can hardly let her out of my sight, I'm so happy every time I clap eyes on her. She finally kicked me out of her house and said if I didn't go back to my place, she was going to call the police and have me evicted."

Donna giggled.

He gazed up at the tree, which stood twinkling above them. "So about this gift."

"You didn't need to do that. I didn't get you anything."

He turned her to face him. "Yes, you did, Donna. I've had a lot of time to think since we found Pauline." His expression grew serious, his eyes brimming with deep emotion. "I've been so busy playing the rescue hero I didn't realize that I was the one who needed saving."

She held her hands still even though they wanted to trace the scratch on his face, the gentle smile on his mouth.

"I kept people away, kept God away, because I was angry about losing Carrie. You were right." He took a deep breath and let it out. "I was afraid."

"I shouldn't have said that."

He shrugged. "You had the courage to tell me the truth. You have heart and loyalty and compassion and you are the most amazing woman I've ever known."

She wondered if she was dreaming.

He kissed her hand. "It's taken me nearly getting drowned to realize that."

Donna's nerves began to fire wildly, the way they always did when Brent was close. "It's very sweet, but you don't have to say those things."

"So here's my present." He looked suddenly uncertain. "If it isn't what you want, I understand." He pulled a small gold ball ornament from his pocket. It shone in the lights, the ribbon around the top encircling a diamond engagement ring.

Her body prickled in goose bumps. "Is that…?"

"An engagement ring, yes, with the biggest diamond I could afford."

Her mouth fell open. "You…you're asking me to marry you?"

He dropped to one knee and took her hand, placing the gold ball in her palm. "You showed me what it's like to hope for the future again. What's more, you helped me see how precious each moment is. I want to share all of our moments, however many there are, together. The good ones and the bad ones."

She stared at him, unable to breathe, hardly daring to believe it was true.

"So…" His eyes searched hers. "Is that a yes?"

She managed a nod through the curtain of tears. He leaped to his feet and kissed her tears away, his arms strong and sure, warming her through and through. When he broke away, leaving her breathless, he was grinning.

They heard clapping and turned to find Pauline and Harvey waving to them with silly grins. Radar cocked his head as if he had listened to Brent's every word.

Brent laughed. "Boy, am I glad you said yes. Marco would never let me live it down if you sent me packing."

All around her the sights and sounds of Christmas took on a glittering, joyful glow.

"Don't worry, Coastie," she said, leaning into his arms. "We're partners."

"Yes," he said, pulling her close. "We are."

* * * * *

Dear Reader,

Christmastime is a time of rejoicing in the gift of our Savior, but that doesn't mean it's always a happy time. This past holiday season, some of my friends and family struggled with health issues that sometimes seemed to overshadow the celebration. Have you ever felt that way, dear reader? Christmas is the season when we feel the loss of loved ones so strongly and the pinch of loneliness so deeply. Such is the case with Donna Gallagher and Brent Mitchell, our heroine and hero. As they struggle through their holiday, they must lean on each other and God's providence for their physical and spiritual survival. Recently, I read in a devotional that we have sorrows because they stretch out places in our hearts for joy. I hope whatever your season of life, you have a great big place in your heart for all the joy that finds us here on earth and the immeasurable abundance that is waiting for us in Heaven.

If you would like to contact me, feel free to visit my website at www.danamentink.com. If you prefer to correspond by mail, my address is PO Box 3168, San Ramon, CA 94583. I wish you joy and many blessings this season and always.

God bless,

Dana Mentink

COMING NEXT MONTH FROM
Love Inspired® Suspense

Available December 1, 2015

DEADLY CHRISTMAS SECRETS
Mission: Rescue • by Shirlee McCoy
When new evidence surfaces that Harper Shelby's niece is alive, Harper doesn't expect it to endanger her life. But Logan Fitzgerald is there to save the day and help her uncover the truth.

STANDOFF AT CHRISTMAS
Alaskan Search and Rescue • by Margaret Daley
Injured K-9 police officer Jake Nichols comes home for Christmas to heal, but when his childhood friend Rachel Hart gets caught up in a drug-smuggling ring, he vows to protect her at any cost.

HOLIDAY ON THE RUN
SWAT: Top Cops • by Laura Scott
After witnessing a murder, Melissa Harris faked her own death and went on the run. Shocked to discover that she's alive and in danger, deputy Nate Freemont, her former sweetheart, must keep her safe.

YULETIDE FUGITIVE THREAT
Bounty Hunters • by Sandra Robbins
When the man who killed Mia Fletcher's husband starts terrorizing her, she turns to her ex-boyfriend, bounty hunter Lucas Knight, for help in the days leading up to Christmas.

MISTLETOE JUSTICE • by Carol J. Post
While investigating his sister's disappearance, Conner Stevenson learns that Darci Tucker, who filled his sister's vacant job, is being framed by her boss for shady dealings at her company. Can they work together to clear her name?

SILENT NIGHT PURSUIT
Roads to Danger • by Katy Lee
Lacey Phillips travels north at Christmas to find Captain Wade Spencer, who she hopes can give her answers about her brother's death. But someone will stop at nothing to keep the truth hidden.

LOOK FOR THESE AND OTHER LOVE INSPIRED BOOKS WHEREVER BOOKS ARE SOLD, INCLUDING MOST BOOKSTORES, SUPERMARKETS, DISCOUNT STORES AND DRUGSTORES.

LISCNM1115

REQUEST YOUR FREE BOOKS!
2 FREE RIVETING INSPIRATIONAL NOVELS
PLUS 2 FREE MYSTERY GIFTS

Love Inspired®
SUSPENSE
RIVETING INSPIRATIONAL ROMANCE

LIS15

SPECIAL EXCERPT FROM

Love Inspired
SUSPENSE

When new evidence surfaces that Harper Shelby's niece
is alive, Harper doesn't expect it to endanger her life.
But Logan Fitzgerald is there to save the day and help
her uncover the truth.

Read on for a sneak preview of
DEADLY CHRISTMAS SECRETS by
Shirlee McCoy,
available in December 2015
from Love Inspired Suspense!

Logan Fitzgerald had a split second to realize he'd been used
before the first bullet flew. He didn't like it. Didn't like that
he'd been used to find a woman whom someone apparently
wanted dead.

Gabe Wilson?

Probably, but Logan didn't have time to think about it. Not
now. Later he'd figure things out.

For now, he just had to stay alive, keep Harper alive.

He pulled his handgun, fired a shot into the front windshield of the dark sedan. Not a kill shot, but it was enough to
take out the glass, cause a distraction.

He shoved Harper toward the tree line. "Go!" he shouted,
firing another shot, this one in the front tire.

She scrambled into the bushes, her giant dog following
along behind her.

The sedan backed up, tires squealing as the driver tried
to speed away. Not an easy task with a flat tire, and Logan
caught a glimpse of two men. One dark-haired. One bald. He
fired toward the gunman and saw the bald guy duck as the
bullet slammed into what remained of the windshield.

He could have pursued them, shot out another tire, tried to take them both down. This was what he was trained to do—face down the opponent, win. But Harper had run into the woods. He didn't know how far, didn't know if she was out of range of the gunman or close enough to take a stray bullet.

He knew what he wanted to do—pursue the gunman, find out who had hired him, find out why.

He also knew what his boss, Chance Miller, would say—protect the innocent first. Worry about the criminals later.

He'd have been right.

Logan knew it, but he still wanted to hunt the gunmen down.

He holstered his gun and stepped into the trees, the sound of the car thumping along the gravel road ringing through the early morning.

He moved down a steep embankment, following a trail of footprints in the damp earth. He could hear a creek babbling, the quiet melody belying the violence that had just occurred.

The car engine died, the thump of tires ceasing.

A door opened. Closed.

Was the gunman pursuing them?

He lost the trail of footprints at a creek that tripped along the base of a deep embankment.

He wanted to call to Harper, draw her out of her hiding place, but the forest had gone dead silent.

He moved cautiously, keeping low as he crossed the creek and searched for footprints in the mucky earth. The scent of dead leaves filled his nose, the late November air slicing through his jacket. He ignored the cold. Ignored everything but his mission—finding Harper Shelby and keeping her alive.

Don't miss
DEADLY CHRISTMAS SECRETS
by Shirlee McCoy, available December 2015 wherever
Love Inspired® Suspense books and ebooks are sold.